HER FAKE DATE FOR CHRISTMAS

CALICO COVE

HAILEY SHORE

PROLOGUE

Senior Year of High School
Bobby

The door to the wrestling room burst open and Marianne Smith came stomping in like a painting brought to life.

Her overalls, hands and part of her neck were covered in splashes of green, yellow and blue paint. Her dark hair curled its way out of the extremely insufficient scarf trying to keep it under control.

"Have you seen it?" she asked, holding up an early copy of the yearbook.

I had just worked out hard and was actively dripping sweat onto the gym mat. I really didn't want to have a conversation with her in the wrestling room that smelled like feet.

Which made me think I probably smelled like feet.

"Seen what?" I asked, using the bottom of my shirt to wipe all the sweat off my face.

"Bobby," she sighed, and I bit back my smile.

This Mari *mood* would not appreciate me smiling right now. She had a few moods that resisted any signs of joy. Irate Mari was one of them.

"The Senior page." She came to stand close to me, close enough I could smell the oil paint and bitter linseed scent of her. Eau de Mari. Sometimes she smelled like heavy duty soap. Sometimes she smelled like freshly sharpened pencils.

I tried to take a step back so she couldn't get a whiff of me, and she must have noticed, her eyes darting sideways to me and then away. I felt my face get hot with a kind of embarrassment. An awareness I never knew what to do with. She made me feel my own skin and it was amazing and awful at the same time.

"What are you still doing here?" I asked, and it sounded like an accusation I didn't at all mean. The windows outside the wrestling room were dark. It had to be close to ten at night.

"Ms. Weidmann gave me keys so I could work on my senior thesis after school." She looked out the window too, as if the dark night surprised her. "How are you still here?"

"Coach Papini gave me keys so I could work out and clean the mats after I was done." I walked over to where Coach had left the bucket with the mop shoved inside. I pulled the mop out and started swishing it over the sweat-covered mats to give me some sort of distraction from everything that was Mari.

"See!" Mari said, her eyes wide. "This is the problem."

"That we have keys?" Seemed kind of amazing to me, but Mari was all worked up about something. Her hair was practically vibrating.

"Look." Mari flung open the yearbook to the senior section. Specifically, to the Most Likely page. The senior class voted on people they thought most likely to become president (Amber Martinez) or an Olympic athlete (Matthew Sullivan) or get arrested (Declan Armitage).

"The Declan one is a little mean-spirited," I said. "Is that what's got you mad?"

"The bottom," she said and pointed at the Best/Biggest section. Biggest flirt. Best smile...etc. Standard high school stuff.

"I don't..." I trailed off when I saw my name. Not under the category of Most Likely to become town Sheriff. Which was my plan. "Biggest Goody Two-Shoes."

"Yeah. They voted us Biggest Goody Two-Shoes," she said, like it was a shock.

I blinked at Mari. Mari blinked at me.

"Well, I am going to the police academy," I said. "And you-"

"And I what?" she asked, crossing her arms over her overalls. She wore a tank top under them and I absolutely did not look at where her arms had fallen. Or her boobs. Her body at all. She was a floating head.

A beautiful irate floating head.

"You're always in the art room?"

"That makes me a goody two-shoes?"

"It makes you too busy to get in trouble." It also made her too fascinating, too cool, too everything in my opinion. "You're off to art school in New York, Mari. New freaking York. Who cares what the Calico Cove Senior Class thinks?"

"I don't care what everyone thinks. I'm upset because... it's true. It is true, Bobby. For me at least. I've been so focused on what I want to do with my life that I haven't really... done anything."

That rang a strange bell in my head. I'd wanted to be a police officer, much to my parent's chagrin, since I was in the fifth grade and Sheriff Pollier spoke at a school assembly. He'd said his job wasn't to punish people, but to protect them.

It was his job to take care of this town.

Ever since then, I'd been thinking about the academy and taking care of Calico Cove.

Every move I made served that purpose.

"At least you went to prom," Mari grumbled.

"You said you didn't want to go!" I said. Maybe too fast.

I hadn't asked her myself, only because I'd watched her tell Luka Daniels in the hallway between classrooms she absolutely didn't want to go to prom. At least a dozen people had seen that particular slasher film.

"You said you wouldn't be caught dead at that stupid waste of time," I reminded her.

"I said that?"

"Exact words."

Poor Luka had been so embarrassed he'd called her a bitch before he'd stomped off. So of course, I had to have a few words with him about his manners around women.

Not that Mari knew about that. She'd hate it if she did.

"Well, maybe I was wrong. Maybe...maybe I should have gone."

"You didn't miss much," I said. "You know what happened to me at prom?"

"You got drunk and had sex with Caroline in a hotel room?"

"Is that what you heard?" I asked, shocked and outraged on my date's behalf.

"No. But, that's what they do in the movies," she said, lifting a single shoulder. "I guess I just assumed."

"I drove people home. I drove drunk Luka, drunk Dec and the entire drunk wrestling team home. Caroline passed out in the back seat of the car and I drove her home too. I basically spent the night as the designated driver for our entire senior class."

She looked like she wanted to laugh. And fine. She could laugh. It was funny. If you weren't the one doing the driving and not being with the girl you really wanted to be with.

"You really are a nice guy, Bobby."

"You say that like it's a bad thing. You're pretty nice, too."

"Ha!" she snorted.

Okay, she wasn't. Not really. Not to everyone. To everyone else she was sharp and hyper focused on her goals.

Only I knew that deep down she was really sweet. But you had to work hard to get to that layer. It was like she only showed the soft parts of herself to people who earned it.

I loved that about her.

"Don't you want to see what it's like though?" she asked. "I mean, before you go away to the academy. Don't you want a glimpse of what's so fun about being bad?"

No. I did not. But I could see where she was going with this.

"You want a walk on the wild side before you settle down in art school," I assumed.

"Yeah, I mean, artists are supposed to live, you know. Experience things so we can use it as part of our craft. We're supposed to squeeze every bit of juice out of life, so we can serve the art. What have I done? What juice have I got? None. I have no juice. I am juiceless."

She looked at me like I should have an answer.

"Uh...you got in trouble in third grade for stealing-"

"Art supplies. That doesn't count. I thought art supplies

were like library books and everyone could just take them when they needed something."

"You broke into the boy's locker room this year."

I wasn't sure why I said it. That memory had never been spoken of between us. Mostly, I tried not to even think about it. It happened at the beginning of the year. She'd been on a rampage about the wrestling team using her oil paints to decorate their faces before a wrestling match.

She'd stormed into the locker room, but instead of catching the team in war paint, it had just been me there. Naked. Like all the way naked. Like my dick was in the breeze.

She'd looked at my face – paint free of course – I would never steal her supplies.

Then at my dick.

Then she'd run out of there.

Yes, Mari has seen my dick.

Every time I thought about it my dick wanted another moment in the spotlight.

"That was... hardly..." she coughed, looked away. "I mean...I didn't *do* anything. I never *do* anything."

You could have. If you'd wanted to. I would have let you do anything.

"What about sex?" she asked suddenly. Only it wasn't really sudden because I'd just reminded her that she'd seen my dick.

Her face was bright red, but she was looking me square in the eyes.

"What about it?" I had to press the mop handle against my dick so I wouldn't get a boner in my sweatpants.

"Have you done it?"

My whole body was going to burst into flames. "No."

She rolled her eyes dramatically and threw her hands in

the air. "Oh my god, they should have just called us Most Likely to Stay Virgins our Whole Life. Are you like, waiting for marriage or something?"

I'm waiting for you.

"No," I said. "I'm just…"

"I'm doing it all," she said, cutting me off.

I was grateful because I had no idea how I was going to finish that particular thought without revealing more of myself to Mari than I wanted.

"Doing all what?"

"All the things I'm not supposed to. I'm going to get drunk and smoke cigarettes and weed. Maybe more."

"More? What does that mean?"

"I don't know what that means! It means all the things we can't even think of right now. That's the point. You in, Mr. Goody Two-Shoes?"

Well, I couldn't let her do this stuff alone. Or with some other guy who might take advantage of her. This was Mari. It was a no-brainer.

"Okay. I'm in."

1

Present Day
Mari

Bang. Bang. Bang.
I knew what the knock on the door meant. There was only one kind of person who knocked on apartment doors like that – the heat. The fuzz. The law.

In Calico Cove – that was Bobby Tanner.

I gave Fleabag a little head scratch and set him down on the ottoman. Fleabag circled three times, laid down and gave a mighty roar of displeasure.

"I know," I told him. "But what am I supposed to do?"

Fleabag meowed back at me.

"If I don't let him in, he'll keep knocking."

Fleabag meowed again, in agreement.

"You could go, you know? Out the way you came in? That would be helpful."

Fleabag flopped over on his side, his half-tail swishing as best it could.

Yeah. He wasn't going to leave. I was giving him the good stuff and he liked it.

Fleabag lifted his leg and licked his privates.

"Right. This is your fault, you know," I told him. "I'm doing this for you. Fighting for your freedom. Your rights." Fleabag twitched his half-ear. Glared at me with his one eye. I picked up his collar, the stupid one with the bell and the little silver plate that said Wallace on it, and put it in the pocket of my skirt.

Hiding the evidence.

Another knock. Louder this time. Like he was a cop and he meant it.

"Jeez Louise, keep your pants on," I said, and flung open the door to reveal Sheriff Bobby Tanner. His blonde hair was swept back and his chest filled out his uniform like he was an actor playing a cop on tv. But he was the real deal. Kind. Decent. Moral.

Looking at me like I had disappointed him. Again.

"Sheriff Tanner," I said, in my most law-abiding voice.

"Mari," he sighed. "Can we not do this?" he wore a shearling coat with the collar turned up against the early December cold in Maine. Which was significant. He was significant. Broad and tall. Blond and serious.

Incorruptible.

Which made me want to corrupt him so bad.

"You're here in an official capacity, correct?" I asked. "As sheriff. You're managing a complaint of some kind?"

"Damn right he is!" The voice wafted up from the darkness at the bottom of the stairs. Joe Murphy.

"I need you to be the reasonable one," Bobby said in a low voice that didn't carry. He leaned forward, smelling like gum and coffee. This was how Bobby Tanner had smelled for as long as I'd known him. His Dads owned Common Grounds, the coffee shop and bean roasters off the square.

Even as a sweaty, sweaty wrestler, he'd smelled a little bit like dark roast.

Which, for me, was ambrosia. But I digress.

"I'm always reasonable," I lied. Predictably, Bobby smiled.

I crossed my black clad arms over my black clad chest and frowned at him. This was how I dealt with Bobby Tanner and Bobby Tanner-related feelings.

With a frown.

If this was a wildlife documentary and Attenborough was talking, he'd be saying something about defense mechanisms.

"Just...give me the cat," Bobby said, the smile gone.

"What cat?"

Behind me, Fleabag meowed, like he'd been smoking a pack a day for all of his nine lives.

"Mari. Honestly, before Joe ties himself in a knot."

"Is Wallace up there?" Joe yelled from the bottom of the staircase, and then the wrought iron fire escape shook and there was the sound of his feet climbing the old stairs.

Bobby, in a very un-Bobby way, hung his head. We were defeating Bobby Tanner's legendary patience. His unshakeable calm. It was, I could admit, kind of exciting. Like seeing him naked.

Which, let me tell you, was an absolute treat.

Naked Nice Guy - Bobby Tanner. All the way naked. No towel. No tighty-whities. Just skin and muscles no one knew he had. And a penis. Well, obviously, we knew about the penis, but not... the dimensions.

They were impressive dimensions.

Anyway, sometimes when I looked at Bobby Tanner that penis floated through my mind and I got distracted.

Such a nice guy with such a big dick.

"Mari!" Bobby snapped. "The cat."

Joe was now standing in the pool of light from my apartment, thrown out through my open door. It was starting to snow. Big fat movie flakes out of a coal black sky.

"Wallace?" Joe said in a sing song voice. Behind me Fleabag hissed.

I smiled.

"Can we come in?" Bobby asked.

"It's freezing," Joe said. "And Wallace doesn't like the cold. He gets chilblains."

"He gets *what*?" I shook my head, regretting engaging with him as the words came out of my mouth. "No," I said. "You can't come in."

"Mari," Bobby sighed. "Why do you make it all so difficult?"

Well, that was probably going on my tombstone. Here lies Marianne Smith. She made things difficult.

"It's a calling," I said through clenched teeth to keep them from chattering. "Now, you should explain your business at my door."

"Joe called down to the station and said you'd taken his cat. Again."

"Well, Joe's wrong, because a stray cat with no collar came in my window."

"Why was your window open?" Joe asked.

"I keep it open to trap cats," I said.

"Do you see how she is?" Joe asked.

"I know how she is," Bobby said.

I stared at Joe and his fogging glasses and the snow gathering on the top of his head, and I did *not* look at Bobby.

And I did *not* think of his dick.

We were friends and friends did not think about each other's private parts.

"Wallace!" Joe yelled again, and stood on his tiptoes to look over Bobby's shoulder. "There!" Joe cried. "There he is. Here Wallace. Here boy."

I looked over my shoulder in time to see Fleabag yawn and close his eyes.

"He's not a dog," I muttered.

"He's not yours!" Joe cried.

Joe stepped forward, like he was going to push aside the wall of law enforcement that was Bobby Tanner and come into my apartment. I stepped sideways and the stupid bell in my pocket, on the stupid collar, jangled.

Joe gasped like I'd taken out a smoking gun.

"I want her arrested."

"Arrested?" I cried. "For keeping my window open?"

"Seriously, Mari," Bobby said. "You have to stop doing this."

"Fleabag-"

"Wallace," Joe insisted.

"Doesn't like that name."

"This is theft!" Joe cried. "Cat-napping."

"Not if the cat willingly walks into my house, Joe. Which he does, like four times a week. I'm providing a safe haven."

"Because you lure him with open windows and treats." Joe turned on Bobby. "Are you going to arrest her?"

"How about you arrest him?" I cried. "For harassment and..." I struggled, I could feel how ridiculous this was. Bobby was watching me like I'd lost my mind. And maybe I had. Maybe I was having a stroke. Or a psychotic break. "Animal cruelty. Cat torture."

"That's it." Bobby threw up his hands and stomped into

my apartment, making it suddenly tiny. Like a dollhouse with all his height and breadth and turned up collar on his jacket. He scooped the cat up under the belly and walked back over to the door and thrust Fleabag into Joe's arms.

A protest would have been nice. A little scratch on Fleabag's part or even a hiss. But Fleabag just sighed and settled into Joe's arms, resigned to his fate.

"The collar," Joe said, hand outstretched.

I resisted.

"It's sterling silver," Joe said.

"Mari," Bobby said, his voice implacable. I dug the collar out of my pocket and slapped it in Joe's hand.

"He's a cat. He's not meant to eat sweet potato or whatever nonsense you're feeding him. He comes here because he knows he can get the good stuff." The good stuff being a can of flaked tuna packed in oil.

"The vet said he needed a diet."

"He's an 800-year-old cat with one eye, one ear and half a tail. Why would you try and ruin whatever time he has left?"

Joe didn't have an answer. Because there was no answer. He sniffed and stomped down the stairs with Fleabag, taking him back to his tuna-less life.

"He'll be back," I said to Bobby, who somehow managed to be inside my apartment and standing next to me.

"Not if you shut your window."

"The radiators are broken, when I bake up here I have to open the windows or it's a sauna."

"Is that true?"

"Mostly."

"You could just tell Joe that."

"That doesn't seem very fun."

"This is fun for you?"

I shrugged. "It's not work."

"You are something else, Mari."

"So I've been told."

I closed the door and turned to face him.

Bobby looked soft in my place. Maybe it was the rich brown of his shearling coat and the blonde of his hair, but he was like a warm spot in my cold apartment with its black and white color palate. I had black and white tiles in the kitchen and the wood floor in the living room was dark. My furniture was all second-hand from my mom, and she'd gone through a real black fabric phase. Ugly, but comfortable. My walls were white and without art, which was strange for me. I'd been an art major once upon a time, but these days all my creativity and energy was spent downstairs in the bakery.

"You know this town is overrun with cats," Bobby said with a smile. "If you wanted a pet cat-"

"I don't." There was a headache blooming behind my eyes. I'd been ignoring the signs for the last hour and it was getting persistent. If I didn't do something now, I'd have to drink a cup of coffee and then I'd never sleep.

"Kinda seems like you do," Bobby said with his half-grin.

"Nope. I don't want anything." That was a guiding principle in my life.

I reached back and pulled my ponytail loose and long black hair fell down around my shoulders. I scratched at the hair at the nape of my neck that had been pulled tight all day. The tension headache eased. "You need anything else?" I asked Bobby, who seemed to be studying my hair.

It was the end of the day and I didn't have to be told my hair was a mess. There was probably flour in it, and sprinkles.

I patted it down to see if I had a pencil or something worse stuck in it.

Once I lost a wedding topper in my hair. A groom had just been sticking out of it for like...hours.

Bobby cleared his throat and leaned over towards the cookies cooling on the counter.

"What are you making?" he asked.

"Macarons, but I'm not getting the red and greens quite right. We have a Christmas themed order on Saturday at The Dumont Hotel."

"Mayor Martinez's big announcement?"

"Yeah, how did you know?"

"I got the invite." He waggled his eyebrows at me.

"She wants a police presence?" I asked.

"I'm more than my badge, Mari," he said.

"Are you, though?" I asked, eyes narrowed. This was rusty teasing. He was the good guy who stayed good. I was the good girl who went bad.

That was the story anyway.

"Can I?" he asked, reaching for the wrong-shaded cookies.

"Fill your boots," I said. He put a red one in his pocket and a green one in his mouth. I leaned against the counter and watched him eat my food. He always acted like what I made was the best thing he'd ever put in his mouth. There was eye-rolling and groaning.

It made me happy. And a little horny.

"You know," I said, post Bobby Tanner food orgasm. "There are a thousand feral cats in this town, why doesn't Joe get one who actually wants to live with him? Why's he got to spend all that time trying to tame Fleabag?"

"Fleabag?"

"Wallace's real name."

"Because that's not Joe's way."

"Joe's way is stupid," I poured Bobby a glass of milk.

"Joe has always been a thorn in your side," Bobby said, taking the milk. He took a sip and gave himself a milk mustache.

He said it all so casually. Referencing our stupid connection to Joe, like Bobby wasn't in that teacher's lounge with me. I cleared my throat and put my milk away, trying to play it as cool as Bobby.

But I knew my cheeks had to be bright red.

"What do you suppose the announcement will be?" I asked. "On Saturday?"

"Hopefully increased snow removal budget."

I laughed. "Yeah, she makes that announcement with Christmas cakes and cookies?"

His cheeks went pink. "Good point. Maybe we're upgrading the Christmas Festival."

The Calico Cove Christmas Festival was a pretty low rent affair. We blocked off the square and had a night of local businesses staying open later. The high school choir sang carols and Lola Pappas made vats of hot apple cider.

"Maybe," I said.

"These cookies are awesome," he said, taking two more. "What's wrong with the color?"

"Saturation," I said. "I want them to look like a Vermeer painting."

"Sure. I like my cookies to look like that, too."

That made me laugh and Bobby reached over for one of the other cookies cooling on the counter.

"Not those!" I said, touching his hand and then jerking my hand back like I was burned.

"What's wrong with those? Poisoned?"

I laughed. Nice Guy Bobby Tanner could be so funny sometimes. "No, those are exactly right."

"They're amazing. What are they?"

"Coconut Macaroons."

"And those are?" he pointed at the red and green cookies.

"Macarons." I gave it an over-the-top French pronunciation.

"These barely look like cookies," he said, looking down at the macaroons that had been stacked and formed to look like little snowmen. Complete with dark chocolate stick arms and fondant carrot noses.

"That's the point."

"They look like art," he said. "Like they have souls."

"Souls? That's a stretch," I laughed. They looked like excellent craftwork, I'd give him that. But art? No. Those days were long gone.

"Isn't that in the eye of the beholder?" he asked, his voice set in a low octave, and I made the mistake of looking up into his blue eyes and getting caught there for a second.

He has a giant dick.

Time spun out and it was us here. It was us in the teacher's lounge. It was us in the wrestling room. And fifth grade. And kindergarten. And forever.

"You know if you ever want to get a drink or something?" he said.

"Have dinner? Us Goody Two-Shoes have to stick together," he said.

It was so casual. So easy that I could have said yes. Friends go out for drinks all the time. Also dinner.

But sometimes when I thought of Bobby Tanner, I thought about him in a decidedly non-friendly way. I thought of his chest and his eyes and the way he made me laugh and the way he walked through the world and that giant dick of his.

Only, I was not going to mess up what we had. I was not going to read his signals wrong and throw myself at him. Being vulnerable sucked. Being hurt sucked worse. Being embarrassed and humiliated was the worst. Nope. I was just fine with feral cats and coconut snowmen and no dates.

"Sorry, Bobby. It's so busy right now, you know? With Christmas and everything."

"Sure," he said, and didn't even seem disappointed. Which made me think he'd only been asking me because he was a good guy. He probably felt bad I was up here all alone kidnapping cats and wanted to give me something else to do besides that and baking.

Embarrassment washed over me.

Could I be more awkward? No.

Applying loads of meaning to something that didn't have much meaning at all was my superpower.

I blamed too many art theory classes.

"I guess... I'll see you at the Christmas announcement?"

"You kicking me out, Mari?" He said that with a smile, like it didn't bother him. He was Prince Charming and I was a socially awkward porcupine.

"I mean, you're welcome to stay and watch me try to fix this color saturation..." I joked.

"Yikes," he said with a wince. "No thanks."

Embarrassment prickled. Right. Of course. Why would he want to sit and talk to me while I worked?

One last cookie and he was across the room, at my door. He stood framed there for a second. The black night, the swirling snow, the upturned collar of his coat – his eyes were the color of a Vermeer painting. That lush, saturated blue. Not dark, not light, but something alive in between.

He kissed me in that teacher's lounge, and it felt like a love song.

I wished I could forget that.

"Resist the urge to save cats who don't need saving, would you? As a favor to me."

"I'll try. But no promises."

He lifted his hand in farewell and vanished into the snowy night.

I shut the door behind him and leaned against it.

There, I thought. Alone at last.

I tried to convince myself that was the way I liked it.

2

Bobby

The Dumont Hotel was done up like a Christmas movie set. Fake snow on fake trees. People in elf costumes. There were giant balloons that looked like ornaments. A woman, who I think was supposed to be a sugar plum fairy, was pirouetting in a full-size glass snow globe.

It was a lot.

It was also...amazing.

As a rule Christmas was amazing – even the entry level stuff. Radio Christmas carols and fake garland at the station. Grocery store cookies. I liked all of that.

But this magic? It made me feel like a kid all over again.

The holiday was twenty days away, but, in this room, right now, it felt like Christmas Eve.

Weird confession – I found Christmas romantic. I didn't have kids yet, so it wasn't about Santa and Christmas morning. I was all about the skating while holding hands. Hot chocolate. Roaring fires. Mistletoe. Perfect gifts.

My stupid luck that the person I wanted to be romantic with was Scrooge McDuck. But hotter.

"Bobby!" Mayor Amber Martinez came rushing across the ballroom towards me. Amber never looked frazzled or worried. She certainly never rushed. "You're not in uniform."

"Am I supposed to be?" I looked down at my dress pants and blue shirt.

"Well," she glanced around at the half full ballroom. "I suppose we'll be all right."

"Are you expecting some kind of mob situation?" The crowd was full of better business bureau people. Jackson Dumont and Lola Pappas, who were slowly changing the businesses in town. Ani Wong who ran the beach shop. Annie Piedmont from the bookstore. Max Patel from down at the fire hall.

"I suppose not," she said, and left to deal with an emergency involving a stuck zipper on a Santa suit.

My Dads waved me down from the crudité station. They did not dress up for the occasion - Dad wore his ancient Free Nelson Mandela shirt and Pop's beard was as wild as ever. They looked like exactly what they were. Two aging hippies. Eating carrots and dipping them in hummus Pop smuggled in from home.

"Son!" Dad said, kissing me on both cheeks, like I'd returned from war and they hadn't just seen me last night.

"Hi honey, have you had the carrots?" Pop asked, picking one up for me. He dipped it in the jar he had in the alpaca fur bag he carried everywhere, and handed it to me. "They're good."

"Excellent carrots," Dad agreed.

"Why are you smuggling in hummus?" I asked, taking the carrot and eating the evidence before anyone else saw it.

"Oh my goodness, honey. You don't know what's in that." Pop pointed at the red bell pepper that had been carved into a bowl and held what was probably ranch dressing.

"Well, you do," Dad said, helping himself to some purse hummus. "All the artificial business, plus extra sugar."

"Sure," I said. These were the people who, when I was invited to birthday parties as a kid, sent me with my own cake made out of carob and almond flour. I would always dump the "cake" as soon as I was out of their sight.

No need to hurt their feelings.

Dad leaned forward, smelling like coffee and patchouli. "You got any intel on this shindig?" he asked. "Why she's got us all gathered here like this?"

"No idea," I whispered back. "She was worried I wasn't in my uniform."

"I like you like this," Pop said, straightening the collar on my shirt. "So handsome."

Not a surprise my dad preferred me out of uniform. My parents had complicated hippie feelings about me having a job that sometimes required me to carry a gun.

Next to the stage that had been draped with red and green fabric, silver ornaments and boughs of holly, a service door opened and Mari backed into the room. Her beautiful desserts on a wheeled service tray.

"I'll be right back," I said to my parents, and went over to help her.

There were a lot of people in my life, smart people, people who loved me and only wanted the best for me. Who would tell me it was time to let go of this thing I had for Mari.

I tried. I really did.

But after she moved back from New York City, she was the only woman I ever saw.

She was the brightest star in the sky.

She'd been that way in high school and she was that way now, trying to lift the wheeled cart over the lip of the door jamb.

Last night she turned me down cold. Like she did every time I slipped out of my collar of good sense and asked her out for a drink. Still, here I was, rushing to help her.

Roy Barnes said I had a hero complex and that I saw Mari as a damsel in distress. He was an authority on that, having rescued two damsels in distress himself, only to be equally rescued by them.

Except Mari was far from that. She was prickly, totally sarcastic, and fully killing it without anyone else's help.

Still, there was something just a little hurt about her. I could feel it.

"Whoops," I said, grabbing the door to help her. "Hold on a second before it all topples."

I grabbed the other side of the cart with one hand and lifted it over the lip of the doorway.

"Well, don't make it look easy or anything," Mari grumbled.

"Here to serve, Mari. Just here to serve." We fell into this banter so easily.

"Thank you," she said, checking her cake and cookies. "This place is an obstacle course."

Her full cheeks were pink. Mari always looked like a punk cherub. It worked for me on every level.

"Where are you headed?" I asked.

"Far table with the…" she turned and cocked her head, taking in the room. "Holy shit, it's like Christmas threw up in here."

"I don't think Christmas can do that."

"Well, something Christmas related did. Can that

woman breathe in there?" she asked, pointing to the dancer in the snow globe on stage.

"It's just a façade. Open in the back."

"This is seriously over the top, isn't it?" she asked. The look on her face was not wonder or delight. She did not seem to be taking in the magic of the holiday. She seemed rather...peeved by it.

Scrooge McDuck.

Why I found that endearing was a total mystery.

"What is the deal with the snowmen?" she asked.

"What about them?"

She looked at me like I'd been surrounded by talking dogs and hadn't noticed. "You don't see the snowmen?"

"I see them," I looked around. Well, there were a lot of them. Were they reproducing?

"It's like a snowman army in here."

"Maybe that's why Mayor Martinez wanted me in uniform."

"Save us Sheriff Tanner, you're our only hope."

Oh fuck. My dick liked the Princess Leia impression.

"I'll push the cart, you walk point," I told her. Another quick half-smile from her lush lips. Mari was lush all over. Her hair, her dark eyes, her mouth...her body. She was curves on curls on waves on curves. An endless loop I could not get enough of.

She wore a lot of black since coming back from New York, and there'd been speculation it was just a New York thing, but as a person who'd been studying Mari's habits since kindergarten – I thought it was something more. Something between camouflage and hiding.

Only there was no hiding Marianne Smith.

Today she wore black tights and a black skirt that was a little pouffy. Black boots and a black sweater, but in deference to the event she'd wound tiny little lights in her hair. They made her glow.

"I like your Christmas spirit," I said, glancing up at her hair lights.

She rolled her eyes at me.

"Excuse me," she said, coming between the small crowd that was gathering. "Cake coming through. Make way for cake."

"Oh my gosh!" Mayor Martinez practically ran up. "Mari, you have completely outdone yourself. This is all so gorgeous."

The cake was a stack of richly wrapped presents with twirling ribbon and shiny bows. The snowmen cookies were there too, with their carrot noses and soulful eyes.

"Thank you," Mari said, like it was nothing. Like this cake and her cookies weren't their own kind of magic. "Let me just get this all on the table."

"Of course. Let me go grab Levi from the paper so he can get some pictures of this."

Levi O'Rourke.

My joyful Christmas spirit plummeted.

That guy. I saw him every month at poker and he was kind of a mystery.

He'd moved to town a few years ago – some big deal photographer who'd won a Pulitzer or some shit.

Whatever.

I didn't love the way Mari looked at him. Like they had some deep art connection.

He had a man bun. I mean... weren't those outlawed by now? Or at least pronounced uncool or something?

Levi did some work for the local paper and for Mayor Martinez when she needed better pictures than what she could take with her phone. That he was actually a pretty good guy was only salt in the wound.

"Mayor Martinez seems...pumped," Mari said, watching our high school classmate work the room.

"That's an understatement."

The music shifted to another Christmas carol. Something bluesy. I wanted to push aside this cake and dance with Mari. In fact, I had a growing list of Christmas things I wanted to do with her.

Maybe I needed an intervention or something. A 12 Step Program to get over this girl.

"Hey, can you help me lift the cake onto the table?" she asked.

"Of course. On three?"

We got the present cake on the table and she was arranging her coconut macaroon snowmen next to it.

"Where are the red and green cookies?" I asked.

"I couldn't get the color right."

"So you scrapped them?" I asked. "They were delicious."

"I think you are easy to please," she said, watching me out of the corner of her eye.

You have no idea.

My parents shuffled up, thankfully the hummus returned to the Alpaca fur bag for now.

"Mari, how do you do this?" Pop leaned so close to the cake I was scared he might lick it. Even though he hadn't let refined sugar past his lips in thirty years.

"The magic of fondant," Mari said with a smile. "Hello Ed and Bruce."

The threesome exchanged hugs and kisses and it made something in my chest sing when I saw the people I loved together.

"You are such an artist, honey," Pop said. "You really are. This is just... well, it's beautiful, isn't it?"

"It is," I agreed.

Of course, along came Levi O'Rourke with his hair and his half-unbuttoned shirt and the silver necklaces on rawhide around his neck. I mean... did he think he was Brad Pitt?

"Speaking of artists," Dad said, shaking Levi's hand.

"Good to see you, Ed, Bruce." Levi said with an expression that seemed to indicate a smile, more than actually being a smile. He was too cool for things like smiling.

"You know, Bobby could have been an artist," Pop said.

"Oh my god, Pop," I moaned.

"An artist? The sheriff?" Levi asked, clapping me on the shoulder. Undoubtedly this would come back to haunt me at next month's poker game. "I find this very hard to believe."

"Tell him about the award, Bruce," Mari said, egging Pop on. For which I promised endless retribution with my eyes. She smothered her smile.

"It's true. He's a poet. Or he could have been a poet. He won an award in high school. We have the certificate on the wall at home."

"You're the only parent in the world who would rather have a starving artist poet for a son than a gainfully employed sheriff," I grumbled.

"I can't imagine that's true," Pop said. "The world needs more poets."

"Not to rain on the Sheriff's poetry parade, but I need to take some pictures of this beautiful work Mari's done," Levi said, with far too much charm. I wondered sometimes if Levi had caught onto my feelings for Mari and was doing this to intentionally provoke me.

Levi and Mari discussed angles for the best lighting and my parents and I stepped away to give them room to work. But, as it had been since high school, whenever I was in the room with Mari, half my attention was on her.

"Son?" Dad asked, pushing his glasses up higher on his nose. "Are you listening to me?"

"Yep."

"Liar." Dad put his arm around me and leaned in close. "You really ought to just ask her out."

My heart could take a beating, and had, for a long time when it came to Mari Smith. But there was no way I was telling Ed Tanner I'd been asking this girl out for years, in one way or another, and she'd perfected the easy let down.

Ed Tanner was a pussycat and it would break his heart.

One of these days though, I was going to have to take my friend Roy Barnes' advice and just move on. It's not like she hadn't moved on. I knew she'd dated someone in Portland, or at least that was the rumor a year ago. Actually, the rumor was she went to Portland to get laid, but thinking about that made the top of my head blow off.

I watched her smile up at Levi while he said something about light and color.

Yeah. He probably knew what a Vermeer was.

Maybe if Levi asked her out, she'd say yes. As repugnant and enraging as that was, maybe it was simply the truth I needed to move on.

I couldn't hold onto these feelings for the rest of my life. I wanted kids and a family. A wife to grow old with. I'd just imagined doing all of that with Mari.

Mayor Martinez stepped onto the stage and walked over to the microphone that had been set up. She smiled out into the crowd and there was a cheer and applause. Amber was excellent for this town, pulling us into the modern world. In her vision, we were more than just lobster fishing and summer tourism. She was making this town see it, too.

Mari came to stand beside me. I fought the urge to take a tiny step to the side so my shoulder could brush hers. Like we were in high school all over again.

Get over it, Tanner.

On the stage, people dressed in black wheeled the woman dancing in the snow globe out of the way and in rolled more snowmen. Snowmen made out of fake bushes and glass and... I tilted my head.

"Are those balls of yarn?" I asked Mari.

"I'm telling you. The snowmen are coming for us," Mari said, the light sparkling in her eyes.

"Hello, everyone," Amber said, smiling out at the crowd. "I'm so happy to see you all here today. The town of Calico Cove has a very special announcement."

There were rumblings behind me and I turned to see the room had filled up with more people. There were tv cameras in the back and journalists from stations as far away as Boston.

I caught Mari's eye and she lifted an eyebrow. I shook my head and shrugged.

What is going on?

No idea.

Levi kept taking pictures.

Beside the stage there were a few people in suits with Christmas adornments; red ties, bits of tinsel. The odd Santa hat.

"For the last few months, location scouts have been touring Maine looking for the perfect setting for a new Holiday, Heart and Home movie," Mayor Martinez said.

"Gag," Mari whispered.

"Oh," Pop said. "I love those movies."

Dad and I shared a very private eye roll. Starting December 1st my aging hippie, anti-consumerism father lost his mind for Christmas movies. It was like watching a health guru smoke a pack of cigarettes. But as Pop said every year, he was a romantic and there was nothing wrong with romance.

"And," the Mayor continued. "I am thrilled to announce that the Holiday, Heart and Home team has picked Calico Cove as the setting for their next film – Snowman Magic. About a single woman who creates a snowman, imbued with all the characteristics she wants in a man, and that night, thanks to the magic of the holiday season, her creation comes to life."

There was a moment of silence as everyone processed this, and then the room erupted in applause.

"Is this real?" Mari asked. "Are we being pranked?"

"I think it's real," I said, watching the reaction in the crowd. "I hope it's real. It's great for the town."

"It explains the snowmen."

This was a game changer. I was going to need to schedule meetings to talk about security, by-laws and permit registration that needed to get started now.

"The movie will be filmed this summer," Mayor Martinez continued. "No one wants to contend with production in a Maine winter," she paused for laughter and the crowd obliged. "But we are using this holiday season to make a very special Calico Cove connection to this movie. Staring in the movie as Grace Halloway, Calico Cove's very own – Carrie Piedmont."

Oh, that caused a ripple through the crowd. Then when Carrie herself stepped out from behind the stage curtains – a thunderous applause. Carrie was a local girl who left town and hit it big in movies and television. For a woman who'd starred opposite Tom Cruise, this seemed like a strange step down for her, but whatever...

Pop made a squealing sound and clapped louder than anyone else.

Carrie smiled and waved, her deep red hair pulled back in a bun. She wore a dark green dress that showed off her curves with a tiny red belt around her waist.

"She's from here?" Levi asked, before lifting his camera to take another picture.

"Piedmont Island," I said.

The Piedmont's were like local royalty, living out on an island past the harbor. Even more so than the Dumonts because they had always been locals.

"Starring with our hometown sweetheart is," Amber paused for effect. "The Emmy-nominated and one of Holly-wood Star's Sexiest People Alive - Jake Foxhall."

Jake Foxhall came out from the curtains to shocked silence, which quickly turned into Beatle Mania level applause. He smiled, lifted his hand and then pushed back his shaggy hair. He stood next to Carrie and the two of them put their arms around each other's waists. Together they nodded and smiled at the crowd.

The flashes of phones lighting up made the room bright as day for a moment.

He really was a handsome guy. Thick curly dark hair, arresting blue eyes, a jaw line like a cartoon character. But he had an expression in his eyes that said – *I know, I can't believe I'm this handsome either. Isn't it ridiculous?*

Jake's eyes scanned the room and then he did an almost comical double take and stared right at me. No. Not me.

I looked down at Mari.

"Jesus, Mari," I whispered, and put my arm around her

waist because she looked like she was about to pass out. "Are you okay? Do you-"

Then, like a Christmas miracle, Marianne Smith turned, grabbed me by the collar with both hands, pulled me down to her level and kissed me.

On the mouth.

In front of the entire town.

3

Mari

Was this smooth? No.

Was it assault? Possibly.

Jake Foxhall, who before he was Jake Foxhall, had been Asshole Jacob Labinski. The guy who destroyed me in New York City.

Changed the direction of my whole life.

Changed *me*.

Now, suddenly, years later here he was. In Calico Cove. My home town. My safe space. This wasn't happening.

"Mari," Bobby whispered against my lips.

"Yeah," I said back.

"You're kissing me."

"Just...please..." Begging was awful. Begging reminded me of Asshole Jake. But here I was, begging. Again. "Act like you like it."

Oh. Well. Like someone put a gun to his head, Bobby

bent his knees and wrapped his arms around my waist, lifting me off my feet.

Liked it? This was more than like. This was need. This was want and lust and a kind of madness that felt...so good.

He kissed me like we weren't in a room full of people watching us. Like we were alone and he was dying for a taste of me. Bobby tasted like coffee and mint and I melted, just a little, against him. Like chocolate in a double boiler, losing its shape.

That was me. Losing my shape against Bobby Tanner's wide, strong chest.

Going from full on freak out to calm, in moments.

"Son," Ed Tanner said, and then cleared his throat. "There are a lot of cameras in this room."

Bobby set me back down and we broke the kiss. I blinked at him. He blinked at me.

"Right," I said, nonsensically, and turned away from him. Dizzy and weird.

Why did I do that again?

Asshole Jake. I kissed Bobby because of Asshole Jake.

Amber was talking, announcing the Christmas festival starting this week and how Jake and Carrie would be King and Queen of it, or some shit. I really wasn't following because I could feel Jake watching me. His eyes, like they always were – sharp and prying.

Suddenly, I wasn't a grown woman anymore. I was that twenty-year-old kid fresh out of Calico Cove with nothing but dreams and hope and a stupid heart that didn't know better.

Tears threatened and I blinked them back as hard as I could.

Get a grip, Mari.

Bobby, like he knew I needed it, slipped his arm around

my waist. Keeping me on my feet. He didn't deserve this insane situation I'd just thrown into his lap.

"Bobby," I whispered. "I'm so sorry." Really, where was one of those sink holes that swallowed cars when you needed one?

"I'm not." Startled, I looked at him, at his flushed cheeks and the blonde hair that had slid down over his forehead. His lips...

The world fell away, and for a second it was just us. Like it had been in that locker room and then again in the teacher's lounge.

What did that mean? He wasn't sorry?

I was immediately overthinking things. He was happy to help a woman in need? Happy to kiss anyone – not specifically me? Or...was it me he was not sorry to kiss?

Give me something to over think and I would do it like a champ.

"Sorry to interrupt," a painfully familiar voice said. I braced as best I could as Bobby and I both turned to face our guest. There he was. A foot away. Asshole Jake, smiling, looking charming and somehow kind, when he was not. "I thought I saw a familiar face. Marianne, how are you?"

He hugged me, putting his arms around my back and trying to pull me close. I patted his shoulder and kept him at arm's length as he kissed both my cheeks like some kind of asshole.

It was weird and awkward, and I could feel people watching, especially Bobby. But I didn't slap the movie star across the face, so that had to be a win, right?

"I forgot. You're from Calico Cove originally, aren't you?" Jake asked.

"Born and raised." My voice was shrill. I cleared my throat, trying to get control of myself.

"Imagine the coincidence of me filming here."

"Yes," Now my voice was too low. "What a coincidence. Jake.. this is...ah, Sheriff Bobby Tanner. Bobby this is-"

"Jake Foxhall," Jake said, holding out a hand for Bobby to shake. Bobby lifted his hand from around my waist and I was immediately less steady. Immediately colder. All the melting gone. I was on my own two feet again.

"Pleasure to meet you. How do you know Mari?"

"She never told you? We went to school together. In New York. Can you believe it?"

"No," Bobby said. "Mari never mentioned it."

"Really?" Jake smiled, like a very puzzled Labrador Retriever. I knew, looking at him, that he couldn't believe he hadn't come up in idle conversation. That I wasn't somehow trotting out his name and our connection at dinner parties.

"You know," Jake crossed his arms over his chest like he was going to settle in for a long chat and I swallowed down some vomit. "I was surprised when you left New York City so...abruptly, but now I see how beautiful this place is, I get it. Totally inspirational. You must have set up a studio-"

"I'm not an artist," I said, cutting off his words. "Not like that."

Jake's eyebrows went up. "Really?"

"Well, that's not true," Bobby glanced at me and then back at him. "She's an amazing artist. She did this."

I wanted to die when Bobby held out his hand to the cake I'd made and the stupid snowmen cookies. I'd been so pleased with how it all turned out. Getting the fondant to look like curled ribbon had taken me hours, and Bobby was right, the snowman looked so cute. So real, they seemed like cartoons in frozen animation. A minute ago I'd been proud of what I'd done, but with Jake Foxhall looking at it, I wanted to throw it all away.

"You're a baker?" Jake asked and his voice was dripping with surprise, tinged just a little with judgement. "That's so...*cute*."

That word slammed into me. A reminder of that awful night in New York City when my world crashed down around me. Thanks to Asshole Jake.

Bobby tensed and I knew he was about to defend me. When I was alone later tonight maybe I'd take that out and think about it for a while. Right now, I just wanted Jake to stop talking about me. I wanted him to stop talking *to* me.

I put my hand back, to stop Bobby from saying anything, and my palm landed on his abdomen. Bobby sucked in a breath. The muscles under his nice shirt going tight and rigid. Well, I might think about that tonight too. The six pack under his shirt.

And the melting-chocolate kiss.

"Are you heading back to New York or California soon?" I asked Jake. *Please say the moon. Please say you're leaving this place and being launched in a rocket to the moon.*

"Actually," Jake said. "I'm spending the holidays here. In Calico Cove. Carrie talks about it so passionately that she convinced me to rent a house for the month."

No. Oh no. Asshole Jake here? For a month? Maybe I could get launched to the moon.

"I'm having a little holiday housewarming party next Saturday," Jake waved his hand around. "Nothing big. A little catered affair at the house I'm renting, with some friends from the movie. It would be great to have some local color. You and your husband have to come."

"I'm not her husband," Bobby said.

"He's my fiancé," I blurted, and the silence after my words was so crushing I laughed awkwardly. *Please, Bobby.* There I was begging again. *Please Bobby, just play along.*

Jake's eyes started to go wide like he might laugh and if he laughed I might kill him. With my bare hands.

"I'm not her husband, *yet*," Bobby said and pulled me back against his side. He dropped a kiss on the top of my head like he'd been doing it his whole life and I let out a long breath of relief. "My fiancé and I would love to be there."

I gave him a subtle shove in the ribs. We wouldn't love that. In any way. But I'd made this bed and he was just trying to make the best of it.

"Great, I'll have my assistant get in touch," Jake said. "I need to go work the room. Mari, it's so great to see you again. And to see you so happy and relaxed here. You were always so...intense."

Asshole Jake walked away and I sagged with relief against Bobby, his body warm and solid at my side. But also...electric. Was he mad?

"You want to tell me what all that was about?" he asked.

"No?"

Bobby laughed.

"I'm sorry, Bobby. I shouldn't have kissed you like that."

"Stop saying that."

I turned and tried to read his kind eyes. His affable smile. He was Bobby Tanner, as true and as steadfast as anyone had ever been. Ever.

He touched one of the twinkle lights I'd put in my hair. My tiny begrudging nod to the holiday.

"I've been wanting to kiss you like that since the teacher's lounge."

A huge knot in my chest opened up, emotions pulling loose that I hadn't felt in a long time. Relief. Comfort. Desire.

All of that, if you didn't know, led to disaster.

"Sheriff Tanner?" Mayor Martinez walked over. "I'd like to introduce you to the producers of the movie. They have some questions and I'm sure you do too."

"Yeah," Bobby said, his eyes still on me. "I'd love to meet them. I'll be there in just a second."

Amber moved on. It was just Bobby and me, and this stupid lie I'd told. This mess I made.

"I'll be at your house," he said. "Tonight. After work."

"Okay."

"I'll bring dinner."

"You don't need-"

"I take care of what's mine," Bobby Tanner said. "And as of a few seconds ago, you are mine."

Oh wow. Was Bobby Tanner a secret caveman? Was I a woman who got turned on by secret cavemen?

He touched my cheek, leaving a scatter of sparks.

Apparently, I was.

"Okay," I said. Then I turned to find just about everyone in Calico Cove looking at me, mouths agape.

Levi lifted his camera and took a picture.

"Who would like cake?" I asked.

4

Later that Night
Bobby

I arrived at the bottom of Mari's steps with a French dip sandwich from Pappas' (for me) and a chicken caesar salad (for Mari) and about seven million questions. The most pressing of which was: *Can I kiss you again?*

Followed by: *Can you touch me again?*

I would finish with: *Can I kiss you again now? How about now?*

My phone buzzed again in my pocket and I knew who it was without looking. I'd put him off too many times. I braced myself and answered.

"Hey Pop."

"Well, now you're taking my calls."

"I'm sorry, just with the announcement it's been a bit busy."

"I'm sure. Dad and I have meditated, and we've burned some sweetgrass and I think we're in a much better headspace for this conversation. How is your headspace?"

"Never better, Pop."

"Well, you sound happy. We just don't know why you kept it a secret. We didn't even know you two were dating."

Dad chimed in, in the background. A low muffle.

"Right, your father says he knew you'd always liked her and well, I think the whole town knew that."

I could tell Pop it was all a lie. But he would ask why and I didn't really know why. But I knew Mari would hate me trying to explain any part of her business to anyone. Also maybe, a tiny part of me believed this was my very own Holiday, Heart and Home movie and I was about to get the relationship with Mari I'd always dreamed of.

A guy could dream, right?

So, in an effort to keep this strange magic moment protected, I was willing to lie to my parents.

"Pop, I really can explain everything. Just not right now. Okay?"

"I'm just saying... I thought, well, I guess I'd always thought you would tell me when you were in love."

"Mari kind of skipped a few steps today." All of them, really.

"Will you come for dinner? The two of you?"

"Sure."

"Lovely. Sunday dinner."

"I can't tomorrow." I was going to be working all day and night tomorrow with City Hall. "But next week for sure."

"Wonderful. I'll make the braised tofu you liked so much last time."

I did not like it. "Sounds great, Pop."

We hung up and now on my list of questions was:

Wanna go to dinner with my parents?

And: *Any chance you like braised tofu?*

What a day. I mean... what a god damn, wild and marvelous day.

I woke up this morning ready to give up on the idea of us, and now I was fake engaged to Mari.

Whistling, I took the steps two at a time. She must have heard me coming because she opened the door. Standing in a bright block of light from her apartment, her hair was extra Mari, and she had flour across her face and a big hand print of it on her breast.

I refused to look at her breast.

My whole being was currently about her breast.

It was obvious though she'd been stress baking, and I wanted, as best I could, to put her at ease.

"Dinner," I said, lifting the bags.

"Good," she said. "Come in. I'm just..."

She vanished from the doorway and I stepped into her place which smelled like sugar, butter and cinnamon. Smelled like Mari. Like home.

Be cool, Bobby.

"Sorry," she said, bent over her counter space, taking cookies off a tray. "If I leave them to cool on the tray, the bottoms get too crispy."

"No one likes crispy bottoms," I said, which earned me a quick smile from her. "What are you working on?" I asked. The whole counter was covered in gingerbread. Big geometric shapes and then smaller shapes. Horses?

"Vanessa had this big plan for the front window of Bobbette and Belle and I stupidly said yes. Now I'm making a huge gingerbread Christmas carousel."

"This is going to be a carousel?" I asked, looking at the pieces with new eyes. I saw the way some of the pieces would be slotted in place. "Like a gingerbread sculpture?"

"More like a model."

I thought of the way Jake Foxhall called Mari being a baker cute and kind of wanted to punch the guy. I'd never wanted to punch anyone before, much less a movie star. It didn't sit well with me. But on the list of things Mari was – cute wasn't even in the top one hundred.

"For a woman who doesn't like Christmas...this is a whole lot of Christmas magic."

"I don't *not* like Christmas," she protested.

"Mari."

"What? Just because you are like the Christmas Spirit personified, doesn't mean I don't like it."

"I've never seen you at the Holiday Festival."

"Group singing is weird. Cult-like. It gives me the heebie-jeebies."

I laughed. "There's more to the festival than singing. This year it's going to be huge. The movie people just dumped a bunch of money into it. Amber's head nearly levitated right off her body."

"Right," she said, putting the last of the cookies on the cooling racks. She set the cookie tray in the fully loaded sink and then wiped off her hands. She glanced at me and away and the tension rolling off of her was thick as smoke. "How were the producers you met with?"

Okay. We were committed to small talk. Fine. If it put her at ease, I could small talk all day.

"They were good. Very...Hollywood." I put the dinner bag on a dining room chair and reached into her cupboard for some plates.

"What does that mean?"

"Slick. No real answers to my questions but constant assurances that everything was going to be great." I opened her salad, poured the dressing over it, closed the to-go box again, shook it and then carefully put the salad on a plate. I found her a fork and handed it to her.

She looked around at her carousel parts covered dining room table. "Sorry, this project really got away from me. Are you okay to eat in there?" she pointed at the couch that faced the television.

"Yep." I put my sandwich on a plate and then dumped my fries out on another plate and carried both of them into the living room. She sat on one corner of the couch. I sat in the other and put the plate of fries on the middle cushion between us. She immediately grabbed one and dipped it into a glob of caesar dressing.

"So, the producers? Did you believe them when they said everything was going to be great?" she asked, and I could see her shoulders relaxing around her ears. She took another fry and then dug into her salad, eating all the crunchy bits first. I wondered what she'd had to eat today. Probably not much. I knew what she was like when she started working on something big. It was like the rest of the world fell away.

"There are going to be tons of problems," I said. "Mostly traffic and parking. Plus, the locals are going to get angry about the long lines at Common Grounds."

"The bakery can start selling coffee."

"Great idea."

"And box lunches?"

I loved how her brain worked. "You'll make a mint. This movie is going to be amazing for Calico Cove. Everything is going to get a bump."

The oven binged and she jumped up. When she opened it, the oven released the smell of Christmas.

"Can I help?" I asked.

Predictably she said no so I ate my sandwich in big bites. I really hadn't eaten anything today either.

"Here." She walked back to the couch and held the spatula out to me. There was a broken horse on it. "Tell me how it tastes."

I ate the horse's head.

"Amazing, Mari," I said. Pop used to make gingerbread and it was dry and thick. I loved him, but it was garbage compared to this.

"I mean, no one is going to eat it, but it seemed wrong to make it taste bad." She grinned at me. Our eyes caught and she set down her spatula. "So...we have to talk I guess."

All right, here we go.

"I'm so sorry," she said, glancing away again. Mari was a force of nature. She was bold and driven. She kidnapped cats and she did not ever look meek or embarrassed. And I hated it. If Jake Foxhall made her doubt herself in any way – then fuck that guy. "Kissing you like that-"

"Look at me Mari," I said, and waited until she fixed her eyes on mine. I let her see me. Let her see all the ways I wasn't sorry for her kissing me and how much I wanted her to do it again. "I'm not sorry. You don't need to be sorry. Tell me what's happening and I will help you."

My words unlocked something in her. I knew she was fiercely independent but that had to be lonely sometimes.

"I knew Asshole Jake at NYU..."

"You call Jake Foxhall Asshole Jake?"

"He deserves it," she said.

"I believe you."

"He was a freshman in the acting department and we met at a Christmas party if you can believe it..."

Hmmmm.

"He was really magnetic. Like when he turned his attention your way it was kind of... hypnotizing."

"I can see that. Did you two date?"

"I wouldn't call it dating. I wouldn't..." she blushed bright red, and without the specifics I could only get angry. I stood up, trying to be cool when I was seething inside.

"Did he hurt you? Do I need to have words with Asshole Jake?" And by words I meant, did I need to beat him to a pulp?

"No," she said in a way that wasn't entirely convincing. I was going to shelve the idea of having words with Asshole Jake for another day. "We were a thing off and on for our freshman year and it ended... not great. Anyway, I saw him today and I just," she laughed. "Acted on impulse."

I had a million more questions, but I knew I wasn't going to get anywhere with an interrogation. She'd go right back to prickly.

"That explains the kiss, but... engaged?"

"You said you weren't my husband and I could see him thinking that I was like... throwing myself at you or something and I hated that. So..."

"You engaged us. Makes sense."

"No, it doesn't," she said. "None of this makes sense."

She put her hand up to the back of her head, tugging at the hair she'd pulled tight into a bun. The time for small talk was over. She'd roped me into this and if we were doing it, we were going to do it my way. Because I'd been dreaming of this since the wrestling room.

I walked over to where she stood in the small space between the oven and the sink. She watched me coming, eyes getting wide. But she didn't tell me to stop.

Slowly, so she could stop me anytime, I reached up for

her hair and carefully pulled out the rubber band, letting her hair fall down in wild curls around her shoulders.

"Feel better?" I asked.

"Yes...how...?"

"You get tension headaches at the end of the day from keeping your hair up too tight."

"How do you know that?"

"Because I've been paying attention to you, Marianne Smith."

The words hit her square in the chest and her breath left with a small oomph of impact.

"Here's how I see our current situation."

"Do tell?" her lip quirked and I wanted to take that lip between my teeth.

"You're not telling me everything about Asshole Jake, and that's fine. You will when you're ready." She opened her mouth to protest but I stepped closer and she shut her mouth so hard her teeth clicked. "I'm a patient man. And, I'm not mad about that kiss. However, a lot of people saw that kiss and heard you say we were engaged. Including my parents."

"Oh my god, your parents," she groaned.

"We have to go to dinner next Sunday and tell them the truth."

"About asshole Jake?"

"That we're not really a thing. Pop was a little miffed at me for keeping something like that a secret."

"Miffed? At you? I can hardly believe it."

"It happens. Like a solar eclipse. Rare, but all-consuming."

"Okay."

"You say that, but the dinner will be a little gross."

"I'm not scared of tofu," she said. Bruce Tanner's earth-friendly cooking was infamous.

"And we have Jake's party on Saturday," I said.

"He probably forgot me the minute he turned away from us."

"I already got an invitation sent to me at the station. I stopped there first on my way here." I pulled the pretentious invitation out of my back pocket.

"That's because you're the sheriff. The Hollywood people know they have to suck up to you."

"Look, if you don't want to go, we don't have to," I said. I wasn't in the business of making Mari do anything she didn't want to do.

She looked up at me with a sudden glint in her eye. A fire I hadn't seen in a while actually. It made me nervous. And hard as fuck.

"What are you thinking?" I asked.

"I want to go," she said. "Like...I *really* want to go."

"Then we go."

"But I want..."

"Yeah?"

"I want to be..." she licked her lips and glanced away.

"Just say it."

"You're a good-looking guy. You're charming as hell. Confident and cool. You're the kind of guy other guys want to impress. You're pretty alpha with the badge and everything. Something like that...it matters to Jake. He wants to be a man's man and you are just kind of naturally a man's man."

Could I get any harder? Pretty sure that was a no.

"Thank you?"

"I want to go to that party and I want you to...worship me." She said it with a tone of voice that sent electricity right down my spine. "I want you to look at me and talk to me like I'm the most fascinating –"

"Done." I stepped closer and her eyes darted down to the erection I couldn't hide and her throat bobbed with a hard swallow. "I'll lay you out on the dining table in front of him if that's what you want?"

"I...ah...probably...maybe too far. But we'll see." Her cheeks were bright red.

"And you'll tell me if I need to talk to him about how to treat a lady?"

"Oh, Bobby. You really are a good guy."

Something about that rankled. Like I was the good guy she could use like a tool. Someone predictable and easygoing. When I felt anything but.

"Okay," I said, "but I want something in return."

She cocked her head. "Quid pro quo, Sheriff? This isn't like you."

"You're doing Christmas. My way."

"What?" she asked.

"Holiday Festival. Caroling. We might go ice skating and there will be hot chocolate. Marshmallows optional."

"Who would make those optional?" she asked.

"Fine. We'll have a marshmallow mandate. Also sledding."

"Like...outside?"

"That's where the hills are. Every day. We're doing one Christmas thing."

"You're serious? All the things you could ask for and this is what you want?"

My mind ran away with all the things I wanted to ask for, but we were doing this the smart way. I figured I had one shot to turn my fake fiancé into something more. Like if I could just show her how great we could be together, she would finally see me as more than a friend.

In the immortal words of Lin-Manuel Miranda – I was not throwing away my shot.

"This is what I want," I said. "I'm going to fill you with so much Christmas spirit, you're going to wake up Christmas morning like Ebenezer Scrooge, run outside in your pajamas and start buying turkeys for everyone."

"But I sleep naked."

I couldn't control the groan that came out of my throat. Her smile was pure vixen and it felt like the walls around us were coming down a little. The people we'd been to each other was changing right in front of us, we were seeing each other in a brand new light.

Don't blow this, Tanner.

The smart move might be to step back, give her room. Only I'd been doing nothing but that for years. And she kissed me. When her back was to the wall, she kissed me. Not Levi. Not anyone else in the room. Me.

"Are you messing with me right now?" I asked her, and I could hear how gruff my voice sounded.

She held her finger and thumb together. "A little bit?"

"A little bit, huh? Well, here's the thing, if we're going to do this, this whole *worship Mari* thing, we need to practice first."

"Practice?"

"Yeah. I mean we need to make it look good. Like we've been kissing for a really long time. So no one will get suspicious."

Her lips pursed a bit. "Hmm. Sherriff Tanner, are you about to kiss me?"

Yeah. Yeah I was.

5

Bobby

"It's not like it's our first time. Remember the teacher's lounge?" I asked her.

"In high school?" she laughed. "It was such a stupid idea to try and do all those things in the teacher's lounge. I mean...who does that?"

"Goody two-shoes. That's who."

"Having the keys to the school made us feel so safe."

"We didn't know Joe Murphy had keys too, and given that he was the school janitor, it only made sense."

Yes, we'd taken full advantage of having been given those keys. After Mari had freaked out about being named the schools' goody two-shoes, she'd decided we needed to break some rules.

She'd tracked down a half a pack of cigarettes and I had managed a bottle of Boone's Farm Strawberry Hill. What she didn't know was that I'd also brought condoms because nothing was as optimistic as a horny teenager.

We drank the wine first to work up the courage for the cigarettes. But halfway through the bottle...she'd asked me to kiss her. Naturally, I'd obliged.

"It was a really good kiss," she said, looking at my lips like they had magnetic powers.

"It was my first," I said. "I mean...my first real kiss."

"Yeah. Mine too."

"It's amazing we survived," I said, even though I almost hadn't.

"Joe Murphy almost didn't."

When Joe walked in with a bucket and mop and interrupted what had been the most epic moment of my life to that point, I'd almost strangled him.

Ancient Greek poems were written about less.

"Do you...ever wonder what would have happened if Joe hadn't shown up and ruined everything?" she asked, kicking open a door I'd been waiting to be kicked open for years.

"Every day," I said, stepping closer, backing her up against the counter. "Let's see if we can make this convincing."

"Practice makes perfect?" she asked.

Could you die from charm? From sparkle? From wanting a woman so badly you couldn't feel your feet? I didn't answer, I just took that look under her eyelashes as a yes, I dipped my head and kissed Marianne Smith.

The fear, when you spend years thinking about something, dreaming, fantasizing about something, is that the real thing might pale in comparison. The threat of disappointment was ever-present. Except there was no situation in the world where Mari could disappoint me.

Yes, she tasted like savory garlic and sweet ginger, but on her lips it was my favorite combination.

We kissed as friends first, awkward and waiting to see if the other might pull away and make a joke. But then slowly we worked past that, to something new. Some new, exciting territory between us. I wanted to claim all of it that I could. Every inch of her, every inch of possibility.

Her lips were soft and sweet. I cupped her face in my hand and she sighed, relaxing against me. Her lips opened and her tongue touched mine. It was everything I'd remembered and everything I'd dreamt of combined.

Her hand gripped my wrist, like she needed to hold onto something and I stepped closer again. Until we touched, chest to hips.

Her breath shuddered. My dick ached.

Yes, this was the magic I'd been looking for. Did she feel it? I couldn't be alone in this.

I cupped my hand around her waist, my palm measuring the arc of her waist to her hip, the dip and curve. I measured it like a mathematician. Like my survival relied on me getting the curvature right. She moaned, her mouth opening further. We lost the careful edge and she met me with her own delicious hunger.

Fuck, I thought.

"Bobby," she whispered against my mouth. And it was suddenly wild. Her hands in my hair, I gripped her ass beneath the fluffy skirt she wore. We were breathy moans and hands all over the place. She pulled back for a breath and I laid claim to the tender pale skin of her throat.

"Oh my god," she breathed.

"I know," I said, sucking her skin into my mouth. She tasted like sugar.

"This is…"

"Wild."

"We're so…"

"Good at this."

She grabbed me by my hair, lifted my head and kissed me. Hard. I lifted her onto the counter and stepped between her spread legs. This was the most perfect frantic moment in my life. It was everything...

"Stop."

I stopped. Heart pounding, I pulled my lips from hers and backed up an inch. My skin tearing off in the process.

"Sorry," she whispered. "That...got a little out of hand."

"Don't-" I growled and then swallowed the rest of the words. "Are you okay?"

"Yes. Fine. It just...I mean, we were just practicing, right? Bobby?"

I looked at her, the lush, red-lipped, blissed out vision of sex and beauty that she was.

"Were we?"

Her eyes went unfocused and for a second it seemed like she might kiss me again, but she blinked and pushed me back so she could hop off the counter.

"Of course. That's all it was. Anything else would be...crazy."

"Would it?"

Why did I keep stating everything as a question?

"We're friends," she said.

"Yep."

"And we...well, *we* could never be more than that."

"Sure. Of course. So right," I said. "Why not?"

She huffed out a laugh. "Bobby, I know you. I know everything about you."

She did. It was just one of the things I loved about her. That she knew who I was at my core. Saw me for all my faults, all my fears. What she didn't know, what I probably needed to tell her, was how safe I felt with her. Would that even make sense to her?

"You are such a romantic," she continued. "At your core. You want the fairy tale of happily ever after."

I tried to see the problem with that. "Yeah. I do."

She gave me that look again from beneath her eyelashes. "I'm not that person."

"Why not?"

She blinked up at me. "Because I don't believe in fairy tales."

"Okay." I had no idea what she was talking about, but she was serious and I had to respect that.

"I'm sorry," she said.

I shook my head. "Nothing to be sorry about. After all we were just practicing."

She twisted her fingers together. "Right. Practice."

I stepped closer. My erection was still pounding behind the zipper of my dress slacks, the taste of her was still on my tongue. My hands itched, literally *itched* to touch her again. Only I was careful to keep an inch of space between us.

"I don't think we'll have a problem convincing people we're the real thing though. Do you?"

Her hand drifted up to her neck and her fingers brushed that spot that only seconds ago I'd sucked into my mouth. I could see the hint of a red mark and it made me want to growl like a fucking caveman.

"Uh...no," she said, her voice soft. "I mean, yes. I think we'll fool everyone."

"Good. We have a deal. I'll worship you at your ex-boyfriend's party and you'll do all the Christmas things I want, including dinner with the dads."

She smiled at me and cupped my face in her hand.

Instinctively, I turned to kiss her palm, my entire body screaming for more.

Patience. That was going to be the name of this game with Mari. The good news was, I had a lot of it when it came to her.

"We have a deal. After all, I'm a sucker for your dad's tofu," she said, and both of us laughed.

The crazy heat we'd shared leaked out of the moment and we could both breathe again.

I stepped back, happy with the ground I'd gained today, when everything in me wanted to curl up on that couch with her.

There was something between us. I was more certain of it now than ever. But there was also something that was holding Mari back. A reason why she didn't think she deserved happily ever after. Which made no sense to me really.

If you had a shot at the fairy tale, you took it and held on with both hands.

For some reason she was scared to grab for it.

"Day one of Christmas Spirit fun starts tomorrow," I announced. "I'll pick you up at the bakery. You guys close at three?"

"Four. We stay open a little later for the holidays. Where are we going?"

"It's a surprise. Dress warm."

I was a student of Mari Smith and right now she was trying really hard not to be delighted. Not to be charmed and excited about being spoiled. And wooed. I think it was one of the things I'd loved so much about her when we were young. Her focus might give you the impression she didn't have time for things like being spoiled. But she wanted it. Everyone wanted it.

"See you then," I said. I gathered up the garbage from dinner. Kissed her on the nose. Stole a broken gingerbread cookie. And let myself out.

Whistling the whole way down to my cruiser.

Yes, the engagement was fake, but these dates were going to be very, very real.

6

Mari

Mom was playing Christmas music in the bakery the next morning.

The instrumental kind without the words, and we had a little contest trying to guess which song was which. The only ones I ever knew for sure were Little Drummer Boy and Carol of the Bells.

Mom won a lot of them.

"Here Comes Santa Claus." Mom shouted, stacking the morning's white chocolate and cranberry scones on the pedestal stand.

I added her point. The tally on the chalk board was now four for Mom, and because of one early morning Carol of the Bells, one for me.

"Good one, Mom," I said. I set the hot cider thermos next to the hot coffee thermos which was next to the hot chocolate thermos. I checked my watch. The high school girls who came before school for hot chocolate and scones were soon to arrive.

"Hey, honey," Mom said, and something in her tone made me stiffen. "So now that we have a lull before opening, is there something you want to tell me?"

She couldn't have already heard about me and Bobby and...*the kiss.*

No, it wasn't possible. She hadn't been at the town hall for the movie announcement. Instead she'd had a meeting with Jolie over at Petite III. Jolie wasn't ready to commit to a full time pastry chef yet, so she was planning to outsource the desserts to us. She and Mom had been discussing the menu.

Mom came early to Bobbette and Belle to get the baking started and I came in to finish it so she could walk her dog. She came back before the morning rush and we argued about Christmas carols.

There was no way she wouldn't already be grilling me, if she'd heard something. Right? Or had she just been waiting for the right moment to pounce?

After all, gossip in Calico Cove was like an Olympic event and everyone was looking to medal.

"Mom, let me explain."

"Oh, you better explain a bunch of things."

The bell rang and in came a gaggle of fresh-faced Calico Cove teenagers.

Right on time.

"Oh my god," Charlie Okinde said, his dark skin glowing with the cold. "It smells so good in here."

"Like so good." His twin, Ramona agreed.

Mom smiled at them and bagged up the scones and gave them to go cups for the hot chocolate, each with a home-made marshmallow at the bottom.

"What do you put in here?" Charlie asked me, his eyes twinkling behind his glasses. "Seriously. You can tell me. Is it drugs?"

I leaned forward and whispered. "Sugar, high quality chocolate. Full fat cream."

"An argument can be made that sugar is a drug," Ramona said, helping herself to black coffee. Her braids were piled up on the top of her head, making her half a foot taller than her brother.

"My twin sister," Charlie whispered. "Ruining my good times since 2008."

The door opened again and Sheriff Bobby Tanner held the door for the twins as they left.

I should have known he was coming. I mean, he came most mornings, whether we were fake dating or not. I should have been prepared for it. But the sight of him in his dress uniform sent a bolt of lust through me so hard I had to hold onto the counter.

What the hell?

One off the charts practice kiss and suddenly I was a puddle for Bobby?

"Sheriff Tanner!" Mom cried. She was a sucker for Bobby. Of course, she was. The world was a sucker for Bobby. "This is a nice surprise."

"You better not be here for the coffee or I'll tell your parents that you're cheating on them," I said.

His eyes, bright blue like the sky in a Titan painting, met mine and seared the flesh right off my bones.

My god, he came in here like a fucking *man*. A man with new knowledge of me. And he wasn't hiding it. I fumbled with the cookies I was laying out. Dropping a rum ball onto the ground.

"Nope. I've already had my coffee," he said. "I came in for something sweet."

Was that... was he talking dirty to me right in front of

my mom?

"So...I heard you two caused quite a stir at the film announcement," Mom said, jumping right to the point.

"How could you already know?" I asked.

"I heard about it on my walk." She wore a bright red sweater with jeans and little Christmas ornament earrings. I wore leggings and a black and white flannel shirt. No earrings. She lifted an eyebrow. "So? Is it true? You two had sex on top of the cake we worked so hard to make?"

Bobby coughed and blushed so hard I thought his head might explode.

"That's honestly what you heard?" I asked my mom. She liked to exaggerate. She said it was a coping mechanism. Imagining the worst. Imagining the best. Imagining the impossible. Seemed like a recipe to get hurt to me, but mom was mom.

"Actually, yes," she said. "You know rumors in this town."

"It was just a kiss," I said. "Right?" I asked Bobby.

"Well, it was a kiss and...we're engaged."

Mom started laughing, but stopped when we didn't join her. "Oh, you better start explaining Mari."

"You heard that the actor who is starring in the movie is Jake Foxhall?" I said.

"Yep. Total dream boat," Mom said with relish.

"He's..." Oh God, I didn't want to tell her. I'd never told her who he actually was. She liked his movies too much and I never saw the point. But he was here in town and it's not like I needed my own mother fan-girling him when she knew most of everything that happened. "He's Asshole Jake from school."

It took a few seconds for that to register. Then Mom's mouth fell open and she stepped forward to grab my hand, all laughter gone. "Are you okay?"

"I'm fine," I said, so aware of Bobby watching all of this. I told my mom the worst of what happened, well, the middle worst, when I came home from NYU and decided I didn't want to go back. "Actually, I am fine because of Bobby."

"She kissed me. It only seemed right that we get fake engaged," he shrugged like it was no big deal.

"Yeah," Mom said. "You're going to need to start from the beginning."

I made my way through all of it, packing a few treats in a bag for Bobby because it was easier than looking at him.

"So, you're going to pretend to be engaged for as long as Asshole Jake is in town?"

"Basically," I said.

"And when he leaves?" she asked. "You stage a big blow up, right? I think I've seen this movie."

"I'm hoping we can avoid that," Bobby said. I caught his eye and shook my head. We were not telling my mom about the other stuff. The practice kissing or the Christmas dates. Which, having time to think about it last night, (obsess about it for hours) I wondered if this was a bad idea.

Bobby was a romantic. What if he started having... thoughts? About us.

Probably should stop this fake engagement then. The Christmas dates. And...you know... kissing him.

Only, I didn't want to stop kissing him. I'd just started, and it was kind of my new favorite thing. And...we were both adults, weren't we? I'd told him I was not a fairy tale person. There would be absolutely no guilt if he got his hopes up only for me to completely disappoint him.

Even as I thought it, I cringed. Disappointing Bobby would feel like kicking a puppy.

"We'll cross that bridge when we come to it," I said vaguely, for both my mom and myself.

Besides, I was getting ahead of myself. I hated Christmas fun. He'd accurately called me Scrooge. Was there any way these Christmas dates weren't going to turn into a disaster?

I handed him my bag of treats, just as the bell rang and a few more people looking for morning pastries walked in the door.

Bobby, who I'd never realized was such an opportunist, grabbed my hand holding out the bag and tugged me until I was leaning over the counter. He kissed me, quick on the lips, then again on my nose and then on my forehead.

It was so cute I wanted to gag. It was so nice I wanted to pull him closer and get a for real kiss.

"Got to keep up appearances," he said with a smile.

Then he was gone.

Mom served the newcomers, who were watching me like they knew all my secrets, and I went into the back to get my bearings.

Bobby Tanner was a menace.

"They're gone," Mom yelled. "You can come out of hiding."

I brought out the box of window decorations so I could start assembling my carousel in the front window, but when I got out there Mom was giving me her *I want to talk* face.

"Bobby Tanner, huh?" she asked

"Stop."

"Of all the men in town I dreamed of you being fake engaged to-"

"I just panicked and Bobby played along and it doesn't mean anything."

"It could," she said quietly, and I looked over at her.

"Oh no. Please tell me you are not going there."

"Going where?" she asked innocently.

I loved my mom. She did everything for me and my

brother after Dad left. We never felt anything but loved and supported. And she did it alone. Well, not totally alone, she had a tribe of women in this town. The mothers of my childhood friends, who gathered around kitchen tables while all the kids ran wild through houses and in backyards. But there was no husband to shoulder any of the load, and she never talked about being lonely.

"When am I going to settle down into the arms of a good man?" A question I got on the reg any time I walked into Pappas' and Madame Za was there.

"It doesn't have anything to do with the arms of a man, honey. It has to do with you being happy. Having someone to share your life with can be amazing."

"I have you. Just like you had me."

"Honey," Mom laughed. "Do you honestly think I never dated when you were a kid? Just because you didn't see it happening, doesn't mean I didn't have men in my life."

"What are you talking about?" I gasped.

"Scott Morrison at the paper?"

"You. Are. Joking."

"Not joking," my mom said with a smile. "We had a friends with benefits thing for years."

I gasped, actually gasped.

"He always wanted more and I always held him off because of you and your brother. And... I don't know. I guess I kind of regret that. I think I used you kids as an excuse."

My mind was blown. I had to sit down in the bay window, carousel forgotten. Everything forgotten.

"Why? I mean, why did you hold him off?" Scott Morrison was a stone cold silver fox who retired a few years ago from being the editor at the paper, because he'd started making a living as a thriller writer. He came in on Sunday mornings for a coffee and croissants. Every Sunday morning for years. He was polite, funny, charming.

And I had no idea.

"Because I had you kids. Because your father was such a shit. The bakery required all my heart and energy and I didn't think I had enough room for everything. Your father..."

She stopped and I got up from where I'd been sitting, and curled my arms around her.

"I know none of the things he ever said were true. I know he was an asshole," she sighed. "I know all of that, but sometimes there's a voice in my head that sounds like him and it says – you shouldn't try. You don't deserve that."

I clutched my mom. Because I had my own voice in my head and it was Asshole Jake. I knew he wasn't right either, but it was still there.

"I'm so sorry, Mom."

"What are you sorry for?" she asked, pulling away from our hug so she could look in my eyes. Because it was never enough for my mom to just see me. She had to see *into* me.

"I'm sorry if you were lonely," I said.

She cupped my face in her calloused hands, strong and slightly disfigured from hard years of kneading bread.

"Hmm. Then don't repeat my mistakes," she whispered. "There's room for everything you want in your life. You just have to be brave enough to want it."

Brave enough.

Funny, but brave wasn't something I'd ever called myself. I kind of wore my aloofness as a false bravery. Hiding from people inside of it. Keeping myself safe from perceived threats. Not wanting anything, meant I couldn't be embarrassed again. Couldn't be hurt again.

"Bobby Tanner," she said. "is one of the good ones. He won't hurt you. Not like Asshole Jake did."

"What if I'm the one? What if I'm Asshole Mari and I hurt Bobby?"

"Yeah, don't do that."

The bell rang again and this utterly wild mother daughter moment was over. I went back to cleaning up the front display window and Mom served up the last of the pumpkin muffins to some students rushing to school.

Nothing was different. Really.

But it kind of felt like everything was.

7

Bobby

My day was spent managing the permits and planning for the Christmas Festival on the square. The traffic notifications would go up tomorrow and the event was going to start on Friday. The movie crowd was setting up a booth to hand out promotional material and free hot chocolate to anyone who stopped by. Jake and Carrie would be crowned Santa's Ambassadors and would be around for handshaking and photo ops.

The various choirs around town would be singing each night on the steps of City Hall. The Methodist Church was already plotting to take the prime spot away from the high school madrigals and I was staying out of that fight.

There was going to be a lot of regional press. I reminded Alice in the permit department that the news vans needed parking permits and she was going to need to be firm with them.

Alice loved being firm. It was like slipping the collar off a guard dog.

Now, after all that...

Christmas Date #1 with Mari.

Walking past the front of the bakery, I saw Mari in the window. She was framed by that spray foam on the edges of the glass and beautiful silver and white balls she'd hung from the small ceiling of the bay window. She was using a measuring tape to determine the size of the shelf inside the bay.

I knocked on the glass gently trying not to startle her, and she still jumped. The measuring tape snapped shut and that startled her again. Through the glass I watched her laugh, which made me smile. She pointed to the front door of the bakery and met me there to unlock it.

"Hey," I said, worried our date was about to be put aside by whatever had her frowning when she looked at the bay window. "Everything all right?"

"Totally," she said, blowing a wayward curl off her forehead. "I had this fear I'd measured all wrong and my carousel was going to be too big. But I didn't."

"When are you setting it up?" I asked.

"Vanessa is coming over tomorrow night. Fingers crossed." She looked so excited.

"Do you need help?"

"I don't think so," she said. "It should be really straightforward. Vanessa is a pro at this stuff."

It was a tiny hit that she didn't see my offer was an invitation to spend more time together, but I knew this was going to be a challenge.

"So!" she smiled at me as she pulled her winter jacket off

the coat rack by the door. "What is this mystery date we're going on?"

"I don't know. That's why it's a mystery," I told her, opening the front door for her.

"For you too?" she asked, eyes wide. "I'm pretty sure that's not how this works."

"Trust me," I said. "I know what I'm doing."

She stopped on the sidewalk, in the pool of light from the bay window. Snow was falling and covering her hair in beautiful sparkles. "I do trust you, Bobby," she said and I blinked, stunned a little by the admission.

"Thanks."

"But I don't do axe throwing. It's dumb and my shoulder always hurts the next day."

"I know. Why does everyone want to throw axes all the time? Like are they working out some inner anger?"

"Right?"

"Well, we will be using an axe. But we're not throwing it anywhere. Or at least we shouldn't be."

"Have I ever done anything to indicate to you I know how to use an axe?"

I opened my truck door and she climbed into the passenger seat. I didn't want to think about how good she looked there in my old wood-paneled Bronco. But she looked just right.

"Stop looking at me like that," she said, fiddling with her bright red mittens that matched her bright red hat.

"How am I looking at you?"

"You know," she said.

Like I've been dreaming about kissing you? Like I woke up hard and had to fuck my fist? Twice. Once this morning and again before coming to pick you up.

"This is how I look at you now," I said, getting into the truck next to her. "Get used to it."

Man, I was really coming up with some great one-liners. I was never this smooth.

I got behind the wheel and we headed to the west, out of town to Daniel's Farm. Daniel grew everything. His place was where everyone in town went to get their blueberries in summer, pumpkins and apples in the fall and Christmas trees in the winter.

Daniel loved crops, he just hated people.

It was quiet tonight. Christmas was only a week away and most people had already gotten their trees.

We parked and I grabbed the saw and the axe from the back seat. We headed to the small shack where Daniel did not have apple cider, nor was he playing Christmas carols.

Instead, he sat next to a little space heater and watched the Patriots.

"Yeah?" he said as we approached, his eyes not shifting from the game on the tiny tv. He looked like Rip Van Winkle with his long beard.

"We need a tree."

"Far lot's all that's left," he said, jerking his thumb behind him. "Fifty bucks."

Mari reached into her coat, but I had the money in my back pocket. "My treat," I said.

"Well, thanks, big spender." Her sarcastic answer made Daniel tear his gaze away from the screen to grin at her. Like they were two dark hearts in a sea of Christmas lovers.

"Let's go," I said, and left the shack to hike over to the far lot.

She ran to catch up. "So...we're chopping down a tree for my apartment. That's the date?"

"Romantic, right?"

She was silent, so I glanced down at her as we hiked through the silver-tipped, quiet forest. The only sound our boots on the snow and ice. Our breath frosted in the air. It was the kind of cold that made a person stand up straighter, and feel alive in every little part of their body.

"I've been on worse," she said with a laugh.

"Well, the problem is going to be finding a suitable tree." I stopped and turned in a circle, looking at our options. "This is the misfit lot."

"That one." she said, pointing at a real Charlie Brown Christmas number about ten feet away.

"That one?" It was lopsided and about five feet tall with a long straggly top.

She walked over to it, running her hands across the dense short bristles. She'd have a hell of a time getting ornaments on it. "I love it."

"Do you love it? Or pity it?"

"Stop, it's the right size for my apartment. It's noble."

"I'm sorry, what?"

"Noble."

"What part of this scraggly tree seems noble?"

"It's very straight," she said with a definitive nod of her head.

I couldn't argue with that. "Okay. Hold onto it," I said, showing her where to put her hand.

I didn't even get to show off with the axe. I got down on one knee and made short work of the trunk with the saw.

"How do we...?"

I picked the tree up and put it over my shoulder.

"Oh," she said, taking me in.

"Don't look at me like that," I teased.

She smiled and shrugged with one shoulder. "This is how I look at you now."

Oh yeah, I thought, this was a very good date.

Mari

BOBBY, of course, brought everything. A stand for the tree. A box of lights. Even a star. I wanted to be a little miffed at his presumption. I also had this sense of warning him that he shouldn't be feeling any particular way about me. I mean, this was all fake. We weren't *actually* dating.

Still...the tree was beautiful.

Everything he'd done for me was all so exceedingly thoughtful.

"I've never had a tree in my apartment," I said, as we unwound the lights from the packaging. They were already tangled and his brow was creased as he worked to untangle them.

Bobby concentrating was very sexy. I imagined how he might concentrate on other things. Like, say, if we were to fall back on the couch behind us and he were to... I don't know... slip his hand down the front of my leggings. Maybe deal with this ache between my legs I'd had since his little Paul Bunyan moment with the tree at Daniel's.

"Mari?"

"Hmm? Sorry," I shook my head and focused on Bobby. Real Bobby. Not hand down my pants imagination Bobby.

"Plug in the lights?" he said, smiling at me like he knew what I was thinking.

I did as he asked and the multi-colored lights illuminated my little apartment. Throwing red and purple and gold light everywhere.

We stood on either side of the tree, handing the coil of lights to each other as we wrapped them from the bottom to the top of my little misfit tree. We had more lights than tree.

"It looks like a disco ball," he said.

"I love it." I did. I was surprised by how much I loved it. We did Christmas in the store. No tree obviously, the pine needles would get everywhere. Mom had a big tree at home, but I just never did one for the apartment. "Really, Bobby..." I reached out for his hand and squeezed it. "Thank you."

He took the not at all subtle hint I was giving him and pulled on my hand, bringing me towards him. When I say I went willingly, I mean, *willingly.*

"My pleasure," he said. "Now that we've completed my activity for the night, we should probably go back to your assignment."

"My assignment?"

"Yeah. Driving your ex crazy. We're definitely going to need some more *practice.*"

"*Practice,*" I repeated in the same tone, now that my stomach was filled with butterflies.

He bent his head towards mine. "I really believe in *practice.*"

Okay, no lie. I'd been thinking about his kiss. His mouth. His lips...

The tree shook.

We both looked at it.

It shook again.

"Oh no," Bobby said.

"What is happening?" I asked.

"I think we may have a traveler-"

There was a scraping sound, another shake, then something *burst* out of the tree. Something big and with wings.

I screamed and ducked, putting my hands over my hair.

My hair was already a net for all things and whatever that was, I did not want to catch it in my hair.

"It's a bat!" Bobby said. I looked up from my spot on the floor to see him staring at the far corner of my apartment where there was indeed a black shadow that looked horrifically bat like.

"Oh my god," I moaned, putting my head back down.

"Just calm down. It's going to be okay," Bobby said, going full sheriff. "We just need-"

He made a very masculine shrieking noise and I looked up in time to see the bat dive-bombing his head. I would laugh about this a lot later, but in this moment it was full on fear factor.

"Get the window!" he cried, trying to swat at the bat who seemed to think Bobby's big blonde head was some kind of beacon.

I army crawled across the floor to the kitchen area, pulled myself up by the counter, and threw open the window. Only to let in Fleabag who'd apparently been waiting for my return.

He meowed at me in anger for having been kept outside so long.

"Fleabag! No-"

The bat, seeing another member of the animal kingdom, gave up on Bobby's head and swooped down on Fleabag. Who went absolutely cat-crazy on our flying intruder. Hissing and swiping, he jumped up off the counter like he might catch the bat midair.

"Fleabag! No!" I cried. Bats probably had rabies. Joe Murphy would for sure have me arrested if Fleabag got rabies. I tried to grab the cat and that's when it happened.

The bat touched me.

A leathery wing brushed my face and my soul left my body.

"Open the door!" I screamed, at this point I would move out. The bat lived here now. Bobby threw open the door only to reveal Joe Murphy, face pinched, hand raised, ready to knock.

"Ah ha! I caught you!" he cried. "I followed Wallace-"

Wallace, having had enough of the animal kingdom, leapt into Joe's arms and the bat flew across the room right into Joe's face.

There was a fleshy thump. Joe swore. Fleabag screeched.

Then the bat was gone and the silence in the apartment was absolute.

"Was that..." Joe looked faint. Even a little green.

"A bat," I supplied. My soul returned, and with it a wild bubble of hysterical laughter I tried to keep swallowed down. But his face...and the bat...

I clapped a hand over my mouth.

"It...flew into my head." Joe said.

"Your face, really," I said. I could be dying, at the end of my life, and I would remember this moment and go out laughing.

"It's gone now," Bobby was back to full disaster management. His voice and expression were calm. "Mari didn't cat-nap Wallace. He came in through the window, uninvited. Just like she's been saying."

Fleabag lay in Joe's arms, licking his paws, clearly reliving what had to be one of the finest moments of his life in fending off the bat.

Laughter burst out through my fingers and I tried to cover it with a cough.

"I have to go to the hospital, don't I?"

"Did it actually bite you?" Bobby asked.

Joe raised his hand to his face, patting himself down. "I don't think so."

"You'll be fine," Bobby said. Then, in a completely un-Bobby-like move, he shut the door on Joe Murphy.

When we looked at each other the laughter could not be contained.

We laughed until we cried. Until we were gripping our stomachs. Until I was scared I might pee a little.

"Your face," he said.

"Your face!"

More laughter. I could barely hold myself upright.

"Bobby," I said, and he wiped his eyes to look at me.

"Yeah, Mari?"

"That was the best Christmas date. Ever."

8

Mari

The next morning I told my mom about the bat and she laughed so hard she cackled. I had to fight the urge to call everyone I knew and tell them about the bat-date as I was now calling it. It seemed like the best thing that had happened to me in ages.

My phone buzzed in my back pocket and I fished it out to find a text from Bobby.

> Bobby: Next date. Tomorrow. Opening night of the winter festival. I'll pick you up at the bakery at 7 pm.

> Bobby: Unless you have other plans?

> Mari: I was going to go see if I could catch some more bats, but I suppose I can do this winter thing with you.

> Bobby: I've told that story about 7 million times this morning.

> Mari: Me too.

> Bobby: I haven't laughed so hard since I was a kid.

> Mari: Not since Lola got a piece of gum stuck up her nose at a sleepover and we had to go to the emergency room. No where close to as funny as Joe Murphy's face when he got hit in the face by a bat.

> Bobby: So we're on for tomorrow night?

I wanted to ask, what about tonight? I wanted to say, come over to the apartment again. We'll have a beer and we can talk about *practice* some more.

The bell over the door announced a customer so I gave Bobby a thumbs up instead and slipped the phone back in my pocket.

"Good morning-" I said, then swallowed my words as I met Asshole Jake's eyes over the counter.

"Wow. You really are a baker," he said, and I braced myself. All the boneless, post laugh easiness was gone like it never happened. I was a young woman constantly being embarrassed by her very first lover.

"I really am. How can I help you? The scones are ginger-bread and the muffins are cranberry orange."

He waved his hand, his face pinched like he smelled something bad. "I don't eat this stuff. However, I was hoping I could order something for the dinner party."

Every word out of his mouth was smarm and slicked with poison. I remembered how it used to infect me. The way I let his words matter.

"Sure, a cake?"

"Why don't you just surprise me?"

"How many people?"

"Umm... I think right now we're sitting at twenty."

"I can put something together for twenty people."

"That's the Mari I remember. Always so agreeable."

Oh, fuck this guy.

"You know, Jake I don't-"

"So, your fiancé, the cop?" he said, interrupting me.

"The sheriff. What about him?"

He lifted his eyebrows like he was impressed, but I doubted he even understood the difference between a cop and an elected sheriff.

"It's serious then. Between you two?" he asked, his lips curled in a half-smile I always remembered as being the precursor to him asking me back to his apartment.

"Are you joking?"

"What?" he asked, the smile gone. "Just asking after an old friend. You know I missed you when you left. Everyone was so surprised. You didn't even say goodbye after all the stuff I did for you."

"We're busy," I said, even though the bakery was completely empty. "So if you're not going to buy anything-"

"You used to be a lot nicer to me, Mari," he said.

"Well, I used to think Santa Claus was real. Soooo?" I shrugged.

No, this guy could not get in my head again.

Thankfully, the Okinde twins came in just then and I focused on their order.

Left with nothing else to say, Asshole Jake took some selfies with them and signed Charlie's Advanced Chemistry textbook before leaving the bakery, cake order not placed.

HOURS LATER, the sky was dark outside the bay window of the bakery and I was in trouble.

Real trouble.

Like high school physics and math trouble. To say nothing of muscle trouble.

The carousel, assembled and decorated, was currently on the biggest cake board available, and I could not carry it from the kitchen to the front window. Not on my own.

Poor Vanessa was so sick with her pregnancy, she'd had to cancel.

Mom was at book club. Which meant martini club. I glanced at my watch. She'd be two in at this point and zero help to me.

Call him.

Lola was usually around, but she and Jackson were so busy with the new bar, I didn't want to impose.

Call him.

If I did it myself and dropped it, all those hours of work would be lost.

"Oh my god, Queen of Overthinking It much?" I muttered to myself and pulled my phone out of my pocket. Before I could talk myself out of it, I called Bobby's number.

"Hey," he said after the first ring. Hearing his voice felt warm and soft and comfortable. Bobby sounded like vanilla cake batter tasted. "I was just thinking about you."

"I..." Well, I didn't know what to say about that.

I've been thinking about you all day?

I can't stop thinking about you?

Why now, after all these years, am I thinking about you?

"Everything all right?" he asked.

"I um, actually...well, I could use your help."

There was the sound of a wheeled chair sliding across a

floor and a thump. "It's not an emergency," I said. "I mean, unless you count Christmas baking an emergency."

"It's in the sheriff handbook," he said. "Section four. Christmas baking emergencies. Are you in your apartment or the bakery?"

"The bakery."

"I'll be there in five."

He hung up and I held the phone to my chest where there was an almost painfully giddy bubble. Not laughter. But happiness.

I am in so much trouble.

HE WAS THERE in less than five minutes, which meant that he must have still been in his office at City Hall.

"I really hope I didn't interrupt anything important," I said, feeling a little foolish now. He was a sheriff after all, and this whole movie thing had made him pretty busy.

"You didn't interrupt anything. I was done for the day and thinking about going to the gym. I'm actually grateful you called. You spared me an upper body workout."

He grinned and I had to stop myself from thinking of him at the gym. Sweaty and lifting big weights.

"What's up?"

"Well," I said, walking from the front of the bakery into the kitchen. Where the carousel sat, fully decorated and assembled. "It's the carousel."

"Mari!" He shouted. That was it. My name. Like I'd left him speechless.

Yeah. The carousel was pretty impressive. Even I could admit that.

"Wait," I said. I hit the on button on the small motor

attached to the base. It began to spin, tinny Christmas music playing through a little speaker.

"I tried to figure out how to get the horses to go up and down but I ran out of time. I think if I had one more day. But, we're already so late with it."

Bobby kissed me. Like, kissed the sense right out of me. His big arms, his big chest. He cupped my face in his hands and planted one on my lips like I was precious.

"Are we practicing already?" I asked, a little dazed by his sudden affection.

"No. That wasn't practice," he said against my lips. "That was, you're just too amazing *not* to kiss, Mari Smith. I had to do it."

"Oh. Well then."

He stepped back and cleared his throat. I told myself not to look, but my eyes had a mind of their own. There was something to be said about a man in uniform getting turned on by my work. Actually there was a lot to be said.

"What do you need help with?" he asked.

"I can't get it through the door of the kitchen."

He lifted his eyebrows. "Like it won't fit?"

I shook my head. "I should have assembled it in the window, but I wanted it to be a surprise. That's what I get for getting caught up in the Christmas spirit. Thanks a lot."

"This is my fault?"

"'Fraid so."

"So... you want to go around the building?"

"Yeah, but I can't do it alone."

"All right. Go open the back door for me," he said. Then like it was nothing, he picked up the giant cake board, my extremely dense gingerbread and the little motor.

"I can help," I said. I imagined us lifting it together.

"I got it. You get the door and look out for hazards in my way."

I opened the back door. The cold winter air swirled in and woke up my skin. I held the door open and told him to watch out for the step. Then the small dip of land before the stairs up to my apartment. We made it around the corner of the building to the front. I opened that door and then, before I knew it, he was sliding the cake board onto the small shelf in the bay window.

"Good?" he asked.

"Twist it, just..." I motioned with my finger.

He shifted it in the direction I needed it to go, so I could easily turn the motor on and off. I covered the cake board with boughs of pine, holly leaves and red and gold glass baubles.

"Let's look from outside," he said. We went out into the cold and stood in front of the bay window.

"Not bad," I said.

"Not bad?" he cried. "It's perfect. You made that. You're unbelievable."

He slipped his arm around my waist, his hand on my hip, and it felt so good. So right.

Hey, Queen of Overthinking It, stop overthinking it. Maybe this is just...happening.

So you're just going to trust him? With EVERYTHING? Sincerely, Queen of Overthinking It.

I didn't know if I could. I mean, what did all of this mean? We'd been friends forever. Yes, there had been that one kiss in high school, but it never went beyond that because we both knew we were moving on from Calico Cove.

Or I knew I was moving on. To New York. To a new life.

Until I learned I hated everything about that life and just wanted to come home.

Sometimes it was easy to lay all the blame at Asshole Jake's feet. Like he crushed me, so I had no choice but to come home. But the truth was, I'd missed the Cove. I'd missed my life here and the person I'd been. I'd missed my mom. The bakery. My friends.

The heartbreak Jake dished out only gave me a reason to get back to the one place I wanted to be. Calico Cove.

Now this was real. This was my home. Bobby's home. And suddenly kissing was on the table.

"Wow. It's freezing out here," he said, and we went back inside. The heat after the cold felt thick like a blanket.

"Thank you," I said. "I couldn't have done that on my own."

"Hmm," he said. "Well, I can't do this on my own either."

He kissed me then. Not soft. Not sweet. Not asking permission. Certainly, not practicing. Or for anyone else's benefit.

He kissed me hard. With intent, and I met that intent with my own.

Goodnight, Queen of Overthinking It. Hello Bobby!

We'd kissed enough times by now I was starting to learn him. Just like he was learning me. Like I loved it when he bent his body over me, crowded me. I loved it when he made me feel small and protected. I really loved it when he kissed me like he needed me. Like he'd been waiting and wanting and *needing* me since the last time we kissed.

"Fuck, Mari-"

He pulled away but I tugged him back. "No. Don't stop."

He growled and I added that sound to my list of favorites. He wrapped his arms around my body, just under my ass and lifted me up. I was just a little higher than him this way so I cupped his face and then ran my fingers through his thick blonde hair.

This time I kissed him. I kissed him like I needed him as he walked us back into the kitchen, away from the window that faced town square. The swinging door closed behind us and I hit the light as we walked by it, plunging the kitchen into cozy grey shadow.

He slid me onto the long stainless steel work tables, his legs pushing mine wide, around his hips. I felt the length of his erection hard against me and pushed myself into it, feeling empty inside. Felling hungry and wild. For him.

Our kisses were open-mouthed and starving. He sucked on my lips and my tongue and I did the same to him.

He cupped my breasts with both hands and I fell back on the table, bracing myself as he bent over me, sucking my breasts through my shirt until he got frustrated with the separation.

"Off," he grunted. I pulled my shirt off over my head and then his lips met my skin.

His groan vibrated against my chest and it made my body hum.

"Bobby," I groaned.

I was still wearing too much. He was still wearing way too much. I shoved his coat off his shoulders. He shook his arms, sending it to the ground even while he growled against the lace of my black bra.

I smiled as he wrapped his arms around me. His palms wide and big and rough against my back.

"What are you smiling about?" he asked.

"I like it when you growl."

He pulled the edge of my bra down until it caught on my hard nipple and I gasped. A kind of pleasure and pain squeezing me.

"I like it when you make that sound."

"Make me do it some more," I told him. His eyes flared hot, and he bent down to suck my nipple into his mouth. So hard I cried out.

"Too much?" he whispered against me.

"More," I said, arching against him. He obliged in every way. More of his mouth and more of his body. His rough hands. My bra was pushed aside and I'd pulled open the buttons of his shirt.

"Come on," I said, finding his belt. The back of my fingers against the hot tight skin of his belly. I wanted that hot tight skin against every inch of my own hot tight skin. I wanted him next to me. Over me. In me.

Bobby put his hand over mine. Stopping me.

"No. The first time I'm inside of you won't be in a bakery, Mari," he said.

"This bakery is my home," I said, wiggling my fingers, trying to get closer to the good stuff.

"I want a bed. And I want it to last all night."

"Bobby," I moaned. "Please."

He pushed his forehead against mine. "Fuck me, Mari, I love it when you beg."

"Please, Bobby," I breathed, open-mouthed against his lips.

Again that low growl. That humming groan. I was a radio tuned only to him and the teasing was over. This time I whispered *please* and *fuck me*.

I meant it.

"Look at me," He gripped my chin in a hand that was no longer gentle. His eyes were hard and hot. I went still, caught in his gaze. Embarrassment was cold water down my back. Was this too much? Was I too much? I didn't want to think about Asshole Jake in this moment. With Bobby looking at me, with Bobby's hands on me. But I'd been here before, asking for something and being told I wasn't what anyone would want.

I started to pull away, but there was nowhere to go. He surrounded me.

"Mari," he said sharply. I opened my eyes again. He smiled at me, his lips tight. Between my legs he was hot and hard and I wanted him so badly. "You're beautiful. You're the most beautiful woman I've ever known. Let me make you feel good."

"I thought you weren't going to fuck me in a bakery."

"I'm not going to." His fingers slid from my face, over my breasts, down across my stomach, leaving sparks, starting fires. I was ablaze in his arms. His fingers slipped to the buttons of my pants, and with his eyes on mine, he opened them. I sucked in a breath as he lowered the zipper.

Then paused, like he was waiting for me to say stop. That was never going to happen.

"Yes," I said.

His fingers slipped down between my legs and I lifted my hips, giving him room. If this was what he was going to give me, this is what I would take.

"You're so wet," he breathed. "So hot."

I lay back, the stainless steel cold against my shoulders. Then it was hot. My skin warming it up. He yanked my pants down with rough hands. My underwear followed. I was bare in front of him and he bent down, breathing me in like I was perfume.

Then his wet tongue licked me as he pushed my legs wide with his big hands. Effortless, he found every place that brought lightening into my body. I didn't say a word. I didn't have to. Not, there, or slow or fast. He listened to my body. He paid attention in a way only Bobby Tanner could.

"Jesus, Mari, you taste so fucking good," he said, licking me. He pulled me to the edge of the table, one leg over his arm, the other over his shoulder. "I've never..." he said, and then slipped his tongue inside of me as his thumb found my clit. I jerked and cried out with pleasure.

"Yes," he groaned. "More of that. More of fucking that."

Bobby Tanner took his time, he got creative. He wasn't happy until I was strung out and gasping

"Please, Bobby," I whispered.

"Please what?"

"Let me come."

He looked up at me, his eyes glittering in the dark kitchen. Bobby Tanner was a nice guy, but he was also a fucking sex god apparently. Knowing what I needed, he slipped two fingers deep inside of me and sucked my clit into his mouth at the same time.

"Oh my god," I whispered. My orgasm gathered like a storm. My fingers gripped his hair. Holding onto him as best I could as his tongue flung me into the universe.

"Bobby!" I shouted, pulse after pulse of pleasure rushing through my whole body.

Slowly, shaking, I came back to myself. The table. The bakery.

"Bobby," I sighed.

I lifted my head to find him standing, staring at me, his lips and face wet. He smiled, wiped his mouth, like he'd had a meal and was satisfied.

"Uh...thank you," I said.

"My pleasure," he said.

"Let's go upstairs," I said, pulling my underwear back up. Shimmying into my pants. I'd run up those stairs naked if it got me in Bobby Tanner's pants sooner. "Let me-"

"No," he said, stepping back. Trying to fix his shirt. But I'd torn off buttons in my need to get close to him.

"No?" My deeply pleasured brain did not understand what was happening. Then, clarity arrived like a sucker punch. He was fine with messing around...but maybe fucking crossed a line with him.

Like I'd gone from someone to mess around with, to someone he...

I jumped to my feet, hiding behind my hair. Nope. Not going there.

"Oh. Sure. Yeah, I get it. Practice, right?" I asked, keeping my voice cool. Casual. I was a pro at casual and cool, it had been burned into me with pain.

"No." He pushed my hair behind my ear, tilting my face up until I was forced to look at him or close my eyes. "But I wanted that to be for you. This...everything...it's all for you. I'll get mine later. Let me just..." he smiled at me. "Have this incredible moment."

Like my orgasm was a gift to him. A thing for him to relish and treasure.

Bobby Tanner didn't play games. I knew that about him.

"Okay," I said. Because I didn't know what else to say. He left me speechless. He left me with my walls torn down and my heart raw and aching.

"Mari? Where do you go, when you do that? When you brace yourself like that?"

"I'm not sure one orgasm gives you the right to all my secrets."

"Does it give me the right to one?"

"I'd rather give you a blow job," I said, deflecting with a smile. Though it was completely true. Secrets were scarier than blow jobs.

He kissed me, sweetly. Softly. I knew he wanted the

secret. Because I was starting to believe he wanted me more than he wanted a blow job. I was also starting to realize I might be powerless against that.

"Okay," I said. "Ask your question. I'll give you one secret."

It was going to be about Asshole Jake. How could it not, considering what I'd roped him into because of it. I could do it. Open my chest and let it all spill out. I was a grown up.

"Are you seeing someone in Portland?" It was so unexpected my jaw dropped. Bobby went a little pink. "It was just something I overheard. You seeing some guy in Portland."

A guy in Portland? "Oh, you mean Sam!"

"Sam," he growled, like it was a curse.

This time I had to laugh. "Uh, yeah. Sam is eighty-two and supplies me with the most incredible local maple syrup. Like to die for. I joke when I'm going to see him that I'm going to get the good *sugar*. You probably thought…"

"Oh. No. Yeah. Like actual sugar," he said, rubbing the back of his neck. "That makes sense because…bakery."

"I'm not seeing anyone if that's what you really wanted to ask. I wouldn't even consider it now. You're my fake fiancée," I said with a smile. "How could I possibly want anyone else?"

He pulled me to his chest, his mouth hungry on mine. Like my answer had triggered something in him. Who knew mild-mannered Sheriff Bobby Tanner was absolutely feral? For me. Which in turn made me wild for him. It was astonishing how I could go from braced and reserved to greedy and wild with one touch of this man's hands.

"Come on, Bobby," I cajoled. "Let's go upstairs."

"No. We're doing this on my terms," he said and stepped back.

He shrugged into his coat, zipping it up to cover the

buttons I'd torn off his shirt. But nothing could hide that erection.

"I'll see you tomorrow for our second Christmas Date."

He said it so forcefully, with such command I almost saluted him.

I did give him a cheeky smile though. "Yes, sir!"

9

The Next Day
Bobby

Mari had texted me to meet her upstairs at her apartment instead of at the bakery. She had a slight hiccup for our date tonight. I wondered if she was getting cold feet about going out in public with me and having to lie about the fake engagement.

I wondered if she was getting nervous about the fact that we were basically now real life dating, nothing fake about it.

There was certainly nothing fake about the orgasm I'd given her.

The key to my whole plan was slow and steady. I needed to show Mari what being with me was like. Prove to her how good we could be as a couple and then before she knew it: BAM!

She'd be mine.

I wasn't certain where this gut instinct came from, but I

was trusting it, because it had gotten me to this point so far. Although I had to admit, it wasn't the best look for the local sheriff to be lying to everyone in town. It could come back and bite me next election. But my plan, if I could be so bold, was to be *actually* engaged to her at that point.

It's not a lie if it comes true.

Sure, we had some stuff to work through before we got there. Asshole Jake. This 'fairy tales don't come true' nonsense she had in her head.

Mari and I weren't a fairy tale. We were the closest thing to reality anyone could get.

I knew because when I texted her earlier to remind her of this date we'd planned, she'd sent me a heart eye emoji, and well... I was a living breathing heart eye emoji.

At the top of Mari's stairs, I pulled from my back pocket a sprig of mistletoe I'd bought from the flower shop, and knocked on the door.

It opened but it wasn't Mari standing there. It was Nora, Roy and Vanessa's daughter, wearing a bright red coat, and a Santa hat.

"Babah!" she cried. Her language skills had been slightly delayed, everyone agreed because Roy only talked in caveman grunts, but once Vanessa showed up and just started talking to the girl, her word count climbed. Now she was a regular chatterbox.

"Nora?" I said. "Is that you?"

"Me!" she cried with her arms up, so I obliged and swung her up high. She laughed like it was the best thing ever.

"You're good for my ego, kid. Are you the hiccup in the plan tonight?" I asked her. Because if so, it was a pretty delightful hiccup.

"Hey!" Mari came out of her bedroom, pulling on a

bright green wool coat. She already wore her cap pulled down over her curls. "I hope this is all right?" she asked. "Vanessa has been so sick lately and when I vol-"

"It's amazing!" I said, and tucked Nora against my side. "It's perfect. We will get her hopped up on sugar and return her to her parents."

"Great minds, Bobby Tanner. Great minds."

She wore a bright red lipstick that made me think absolutely inappropriate things about what I'd like to do to that mouth.

"Are we ready?" Mari asked, her eyes wide for Nora.

"Uh oh!" Nora yelled.

"That means ready," Mari translated, though *uh oh* was a pretty inexhaustible catch-all.

"Just a second," I said, and though cheesy, I was fully committed and held up my little sprig of mistletoe.

It had a green ribbon that matched Mari's coat and I held it over her head.

Mari laughed. "Your game so weak you need props?"

"Yes?"

With a smile, she kissed me like I was hers. Like she was mine.

"Uh oh!" Nora cried. "Me. Me."

We turned our kisses Nora's way, squishing her cheeks with our lips until she was laughing. I leaned back and watched Mari, smiling and twinkling, and had to keep my mouth shut so I wouldn't blurt out all the things I was feeling.

"Let's go," Mari said. I carried Nora down the steps while she locked up behind us. The square was already buzzing with people. The high school jazz band was playing Christmas carols on the steps of City Hall.

We stopped at the first cart to get Nora a hot steamed milk and a jingle bell we could put around her wrist.

"Roy is going to kill you," Mari said, as I strapped it onto Nora who immediately went wild making the thing ring.

"I know, it's great, right?" Torturing Roy was a full-time pleasure in my life. He was much less grumpy now that he and Vanessa were firmly a family with another baby on the way and adoption paperwork filed for Nora.

But Roy Barnes was never going to be Mr. Sunshine, no matter how happy he was. It was part of his charm.

"The booths are new," Mari said, and then stopped to look more carefully at one of the ones we passed. A jewelry maker was holding up a mirror to Madame Za so she could see how her earrings looked.

"Who is that?" Mari asked.

I glanced back at the jewelry designer but didn't recognize her. She was young and pretty and wearing a swanky coat that looked like it was made out of tinfoil.

"Someone involved with the movie," I said.

"How do you know that?"

"They don't have good coats."

"Is that weird?" Mari asked, looking at the outsider with some suspicion.

"Mari," I sighed and put my arm around her. "Everything the movie people do is weird. It's like they haven't figured out Calico Cove is an actual town in the Northeast and not a location set in Los Angeles."

"Hey!" Levi came walking up to us, camera around his neck. He wore those gloves that didn't have fingers. Those gloves were stupid, I think the world could agree on that. But on him...of course they looked cool. If the guy started wearing a top hat, he'd make it look cool. "It's the new lovebirds."

"Hi Levi," Mari said. I took note that she didn't make any objections to the lovebird comment.

"Levi," I shook his hand and then put my arm right back around Mari's shoulders.

"Me, bell!" Nora shouted and waved her jingle bell wrist in Levi's face.

"Oh, Roy is going to kill you for that," Levi said with a smile. "I got her a whistle, once. I actually thought he was going to punch me."

"Roy smashed it with a hammer," Mari said.

"Roy's no fun," I said.

"So, you two are making it official?" Levi asked, snapping a quick picture of Nora and then one of the three of us. "I have to say it's about time. The Sheriff here has been pin-"

"Going to keep on walking," I said, pulling Mari with me. She laughed over her shoulder and called goodbye to Levi.

"Down!" Nora cried. The Shah's were here with their two dogs and when I set Nora down she made a beeline for the couple and their extremely friendly, mellow mutts.

"What was he going to say?" Mari asked me, still under my arm. She put her arm around my back as we walked to catch up with Nora, and it was amazing how she fit against me. Hip to hip. Perfect.

"Don't know."

"Bobby," she said, in that *I don't believe you even a little bit* way.

I sighed. Maybe this had to be part of the process. A little truth mixed in with practice kissing and orgasms.

"He might have been about to suggest that I had a crush on you."

"Really? Like a *crush* crush? How long?" she asked.

"Let's not get into this here."

"Why?"

"Because maybe it's embarrassing."

"Bobby!" she said, clearly exasperated by my procrastination in answering.

I stopped and looked at her. "Because I've had a crush on you since high school."

She immediately took a step back. Not a good sign.

"Don't get weird about it," I said. "It's just-"

"I'm not getting weird," she said. "I just...didn't know."

"Now you do. So, no big deal."

She bent down to focus on Nora, who had gotten her jingle bell bracelet stuck in the dog collar, when everyone around us went still and weird.

"Hi everyone," Jake Foxhall said, walking into the group like he was Kris Kringle. He wore a red and black plaid lumberjack coat that was not going to be warm enough. Along with dark denim jeans and leather boots – also not going to be warm enough.

Mari stood up quickly and held Nora almost like a shield. I put my arm back around her waist. I wasn't entirely sure what I needed to protect her from with this guy, but I was not leaving her side.

"Mari! Look at you," he said with his warm movie star smile. He leaned in for a kiss, but Nora stiff-armed him Heisman style and said. "No!"

Jake laughed it off. "Funny kid."

"Sorry," Mari said. "New words and everything."

"No. I get it. It's great you're teaching her boundaries, Mari. Everyone needs that, don't they?" His smile was movie star slick, but Mari flinched like he'd put a knife between her ribs. "And look at you, with a kid! You always said that life wasn't for you. I guess once you gave up on your art you had time for other things."

"Nora's not mine," Mari said. "We're just babysitting."

"Practice, I guess," Jake said. Again I had that feeling like this was all double talk. He was saying one thing and meant another, but the only one who understood the second was Mari. Though, I really didn't like that bullshit about Mari giving up on her art.

"Good to see you again, Jake," I said, putting a hand to Mari's lower back and pushing her into motion so we could end this little chit-chat. "Looking forward to your party on Saturday."

"Yeah!" he said. "I'm looking forward to it, too."

Casually, we walked away. I leaned down and kissed Mari's head and then Nora's head when she insisted.

"You okay?" I asked her.

Mari frowned. "He's just an asshole."

"I'm getting that."

10

Bobby

After a few hours at the festival, we made the walk back to Roy and Vanessa's house. We handed off a sleeping Nora to Roy. They'd redecorated the living room not too long ago and there was a nice sectional couch, and finally a new TV.

I could see the shape of Vanessa, currently asleep on the couch, a blanket tucked around her.

"She okay?" Mari whispered.

"Yeah, just..." Roy shook his head. "I thought morning sickness was only supposed to be in the morning."

"Can she keep anything down?"

"Smoothies and crackers. She's making a list of food she can't wait to eat when it doesn't make her sick."

"Sounds like Ness. Give her a kiss for me," Mari said.

"Me too," I joked, and Roy scowled at me.

We walked back to Mari's place, snowflakes falling

around us. The cold quiet felt so peaceful.

"That was a fun night," she said.

"Christmas Date #2 in the books."

"What's next?"

"It's a surprise."

"Do you want to come-"

"Yes!" I shouted. "Wait. Was that too eager?"

She laughed. "No, you're playing it very cool."

Snow fluttered down on her eyelashes and melted, but not before glittering a little in the moonlight.

"Come on," she said, and I followed her up the stairs to her apartment. She wore jeans tonight, which wasn't something she did very often. She was a skirt and leggings girl. The dark jeans and her ass climbing the stairs were an unreasonable combination. I reached up and tucked my fingers in her pocket. Feeling the shift and flex of her body as we got to her door.

My desire for her, constantly on the back burner simmering away, boiled over, and when she opened the door to her apartment I put my arms around her waist and stepped her forward so I could shut the door behind us.

"Bobby," she breathed. "Is this...I mean, we're just having fun, right? Is that okay?"

"Everything about you is okay," I said.

I unzipped her jacket and threw it on the ground. Then from behind her, I practically mauled her body under the pretty sweater she wore. Her breasts, the curve of her stomach. Her nipples were hard like maybe she'd been simmering away too. I cupped my hands between her legs, and I swear I could feel her, hot and wet under the denim.

We lurched forward until she was braced against the kitchen table, her ass pushed back hard against me. She made this maddening little circle with her hips, trapping the head of my cock between my stomach and her ass. I groaned, pushing her sweater up and over her head. Her beautiful, strong spine, her gorgeous shoulders, all her creamy skin revealed to me.

She wore a red bra.

I wouldn't have thought I was a lingerie kind of man. I always thought naked was better. But this red bra and her beautiful body, well, I had to see it for myself.

I turned her around and it wasn't just a red bra. It was a red bra with a little green bow on the front of it between her fucking stunning tits.

"Is that... a Christmas bra?" My voice was practically gravel.

"It is."

Scrooge McDuck wore a Christmas bra.

"Is that for me?"

"It's not really for me," she said with a laugh, shaking her dark hair over her shoulders, making her tits shimmy.

I was so hard I might never recover.

I bent over her small body, kissing her breasts, sucking the nipples through the lace. Nibbling until she shook against me.

"Mari," I groaned against her skin, kissing down her stomach until I sank to my knees in front of her.

"No," she said. "I mean, trust me, I love where you're going. I *really* do. But I need balance."

I looked up at her from where I worshipped her on my knees. "I have no idea what you're talking about."

"Get up, Bobby. It's my turn to blow your mind."

I cupped her face in my hands. "You always blow my mind."

"I think your standards must be low," she laughed, as she pushed me backwards to the couch. There was something in the way she said that, like I might be happy with anyone.

Or just happy to be getting my dick sucked by someone with tits. She had to know better. Especially after what I'd told her tonight.

"You're my standard, Mari," I told her. "There's nothing low about you."

She unbuckled my belt and lowered the zipper as I kissed her. I knew it was coming, was braced for it, but the second she slipped her hand into my boxers and curled her fingers around my dick, I was barely hanging on. This might be the shortest hand job ever recorded.

She pushed my pants down over my hips and broke the kiss to look down at my cock.

"Swear to god, Bobby, that dick of yours is a work of art."

My dick flexed, preening under her attention, and I bit my lower lip begging whatever god was in charge of such things that I didn't blow my wad immediately.

She pushed against my stomach encouraging me to sit, so I did. I sat butt naked on the couch while she leaned down to take off my boots, pulling my pants completely off. All while I cupped her breasts in my hands anytime they were in range.

"Jesus, can you stop with the clothes?" I muttered and pulled her close, sucking her nipple into my mouth. "Just let me kiss you."

I put my hands in her hair, holding her still while I ravaged her mouth. I liked this angle, her over me. I tried to pull her closer to get her to spread those legs over my lap but she pulled back.

Her eyes were dilated and half-wild. Her smile was gone like I'd kissed her into some other place in her brain. Something wild and on the edge of pleasure.

"Come here," I moaned, cupping her ass and squeezing until she closed her eyes with a moan. "Come sit on my dick."

She shook her head, her black curls framing her face and falling over her shoulders. "No, this time I want you in my mouth," she said. "Let me."

I closed my eyes on a moan, clinging to control. She grabbed a throw pillow off the couch and put it on the floor between my legs.

"What are you doing?" I whispered.

"Getting comfortable." She knelt between my spread knees. The velvet skin of her arms and her waist against the bare skin of my thighs was electric. She was electric.

"Will it be weird if I tell you I have been thinking about this since that time I walked in on you in the locker room?" Her breath feathered over the head of my cock and I spread my arms out along the back of the couch, gripping the cushions with both hands.

"You okay, Bobby?" she whispered, her mouth so close I could feel the heat and the damp of it. "You seem a little-"

My head dropped back on my shoulders. "Stop teasing me and suck my fucking cock, Mari. Or swear to god I'm fucking you on that floor in two seconds."

I looked at her then. Waited for her response. Her eyes locked on mine, she put out her tongue and licked me from the bottom to the top of my cock.

"Like that?" she whispered, like she didn't know I was crazed for her.

"More," I demanded.

It was like something had snapped and nice guy Bobby Tanner was not in the building anymore. Based on her reaction, I think she loved it too.

Testing my theory, I put my hand in her hair, gripping it

in a fist, and she gasped. "Open your mouth," I told her and she did, her plush lips parting over the head of my cock. "Wider."

She made a whimpering noise in her throat, like she was losing it too. I arched my hips, slowly fucking my cock into her mouth. Just a little. Not enough and too much all at the same time. I cupped my hand around the back of her neck, easing her forward as I arched up and I slid deep into her mouth.

We both groaned.

Words I could not stop poured out of me. "So good, so fucking good, Mari. You're so beautiful on your knees like this. Look at you, Jesus, look at you sucking my dick like that. Like you love it. Like-"

She curled her hand around the base of my cock and we weren't playing any more. She stroked me hard with one hand while tonguing the head of my cock. I knew this wasn't going to last forever, but I wanted a little bit more. Just a little bit more of her like this. Flushed and wild and making me feel so good.

"Stop," I groaned.

"Why?" she asked. Her hand still, her mouth letting go of me with a pop.

"I'm going to come."

"That's the idea," she said, her eyes wicked. "That's what I want."

"In your mouth?"

"Wherever you want."

Oh my god. Oh my god, the things I'd never let myself think about. The way I suddenly wanted to come on her tits and the small of her back. All over her ass. I wanted to come in her pussy.

My hand clenched on her neck and she understood I

was at the edge. Leaning forward, she sucked me deep inside her hot mouth and I exploded. Swearing and coming and jerking myself into her. It was probably too much. I tried to pull back but she only held on tighter to my cock, holding me in place.

That she loved this as much as I did, made me come even harder. Until it felt like my soul was leaving my body and I was made of the same things that made up the stars.

"Oh my god," I gasped, watching as she slipped me out of her mouth. Her lips were wet and full. More come leaked out of the tip of my cock and she licked it up with the tip of her tongue. I couldn't fucking take it anymore.

"You," I said, and pushed her back, making room for me on the floor. "Take the fucking pants off."

She laid back and shimmied out of the pants. She started to take her pretty red underwear off too, but I stopped her.

"No, leave it."

"You're going to fuck me through red satin?"

"Something like that."

I shifted furniture around until I could get down between her legs. She laughed as the couch got shoved back.

"The bedroom-"

"Here," I said. "Can't fucking wait."

I wasn't cool about it. I didn't know how to be cool about it.

I traced the edges of the wet spot on her panties. "You did like it," I said.

"What?" she panted, as I ran my finger down her slit, over her panties.

"Sucking my cock."

"Yes," she moaned. I found her clit, pressed harder on it

until she spread her legs out wider, like she was trying to get closer to me.

More things I shouldn't say. More secrets I needed to keep.

So I put my mouth over the wet spot on her panties and fucking devoured her through the silk. She was salty and sweet and she lifted her hips into me. I used my tongue to rub that fabric against her clit. I spread her legs out wide so I could cup her ass in my hand, holding her against my mouth.

"Bobby," she whispered. Then she groaned it. Fuck these panties I thought, and yanked them out of the way, sliding two fingers deep inside. I found that spot that made her jerk and writhe and I worked it. Worked her hard. I could have done it for hours, but she came as fast as I did. Her fingers in my hair, my nose mashed against her pussy. The smell and taste of her in my head, where it was just a part of me now.

This, I thought. *Her*. She was everything I'd ever wanted.

Did she know that? Could she feel it?

I got myself up off the floor. My knees were red, where I'd been bracing myself, and I fucked up my elbow holding her legs out wide. Except if I was going to get injured doing anything, making Mari come so hard she screamed, was top of the list.

I found my pants and pulled on my boxers, then went to get us a glass of water. When I turned around, she was sitting back against the couch, a blanket over her lap. The straps of her pretty red bra falling off her shoulders. She was flushed and sweaty. Her hair sticking in wet clumps against her neck.

"Thank you," she said, as I handed her the water. She took a deep drink and I watched her throat bob. I had to resist the urge to kiss the vein just under her skin and the tender hollow where her heart beat. I sat down next to her, my legs kicked out in front of me. My knee touching hers. My toe touching hers.

The Christmas tree I gave her was lit up with the lights and adorned with the small box of ornaments I'd given her.

This might be the best moment of my life.

"Can I ask you something?" she said, pushing her shoulder against mine.

"Sure."

"If you had a crush on me, why didn't you ever just ask me out?"

"Are you serious? I did! About a million times. You shot me down every time."

She blinked, like we were remembering a different history. "No...I mean, sure, you would say let's grab coffee or something. But you never made it really sound like a date. You were always so casual."

Fair enough. Maybe a lot of that was on me. "When you came home, after that first year of school, I didn't think you wanted anything to do with the male species. Then later, I guess I didn't want to scare you off."

She took another sip of water. "So...who have you dated in the last four years?"

Ah. She figured it out. I took a deep breath and let it out slowly, but my silence gave it away.

"You're kidding me," she said. "Really?"

"Really."

"No one?"

"Look, I'm not going to sit here and tell you there weren't hook ups. But no, I wasn't going to date or get serious about anyone when I wanted to date you. That didn't seem fair to anyone."

She pressed her fingers to her forehead and sighed.

"Even though you thought I was hooking up with some guy in Portland?"

"Hooking up," I said. "Not dating. There's a difference. Now it's my turn to ask you a question."

"Okay," she said, and I could hear the caution in her tone.

"You'll tell me all about Asshole Jake when you're ready. But what did he mean about you not wanting the whole family life? You love kids."

She took a slow breath so I reached over and laced my fingers with hers. It was a marvel that a few minutes ago we were so raw and filthy with each other. Now these same hands could be so careful and kind.

"Like..." she stopped. Took a breath. "I don't know how much you know about my dad."

"He left."

She laughed humorlessly. "Yeah, that's about it, I guess. He left when I was six and my brother was eight. Only when I say he left...he vanished. Mom thought he'd been in an accident and she called hospitals from here to Boston. She worried maybe he'd been kidnapped or something. Or murdered and left in the woods-"

"Oh my god."

"I know. I don't remember it. My brother does a little. What I do remember was, for about a year my mom kept telling me that my dad was coming back. Like if she held on to hope, it might happen. Then one night she got a phone call and it was him. Nothing bad had happened. He'd just... moved away and found another woman he wanted to marry. He wanted a divorce and needed her to sign the paperwork."

"Marianne," I breathed.

"I know," she laughed again, her defense mechanism, I knew so well. "I mean, it was shocking. Mom was shocked.

My brother. I remember how all her friends descended on us. They cleaned our house and put casseroles in the freezer. Got my brother and me to school every day. Kept us for sleepovers all so she could...grieve, I guess. The whole time they'd whisper that this was for the best. That he was an asshole and he wasn't happy unless Mom was unhappy. I think, even at that age, I kind of knew that was the truth."

"That must have been so hard."

"It was. The hardest thing is that I don't even think my Mom and I are that special. Men leave. A lot. Women do too. For lots of reasons. My point is, I've seen the other side of the fairy tale and it's rotten. It's lies and make-believe and a single mother of two crying at her kitchen table in the middle of the night so her kids don't hear her. So no, I never wanted anything to do with that life." She shrugged.

"And then you met Jake?"

She pulled in a shaky breath. "He just reinforced all of it. The fairy tale is not for me. I'm sorry."

She put her hand against my chest quickly, then pulled it back.

"Don't be sorry," I said, taking her hand back. "I don't think marriage, or love, is a fairy tale. My dads have fought some serious battles, you know. Not just to be seen as human by some parts of society, or even have their marriage recognized the same way straight marriages are recognized. They each have their own demons. Pop has a temper," I said with a smile. "And a sense of drama. Their fights got loud and legendary. But they worked it out, every time. Sometimes with a marriage counselor, sometimes with tears. Sometimes with me staying at my aunt's house so they could go to the city for a weekend. That's what I saw growing up. That's what I know. I don't believe in the fairy tale either, Mari. When I fall in love, I'll believe in the person I love."

11

Mari

The next day was what we in the baking business called – an absolute shit show. Our second oven, which was actually our first oven and over fifteen years old, was choosing this moment to take its final bow.

"Mom, the back right corner is like seven hundred degrees," I said, coming in from the back to the front of the bakery where there were dozens of people, milling around. "Holy shit," I breathed, "what is going on?"

"I think it was that festival," Mom said, ringing things up, bagging treats and smiling. Always smiling. It's why she was in the front of the house and I was in the back. "Or the press release about the movie filming here this summer. I don't know. I'm almost out of cookies. Out of scones. Out of hot chocolate."

"I can get more cookies baking, but the second oven is

toast. The left corner is burning everything and the right corner isn't even getting warm."

Mom looked at me with something close to panic in her eyes. I felt like that kid I'd been. Young and aware that things were precarious in our house, but not entirely sure how precarious, or why, and wanting to do anything I could to make things better.

"Mom, don't sweat it. I got it. We'll have cookies in fifteen. Hot out of the oven."

"Okay," she said with a nod.

In the back, we had tubs of dough prepared. Ginger, chocolate chip, oatmeal. I scooped everything onto trays. I got the first batch in the good oven and then ran the second batch to my oven upstairs.

I spent the next two hours running up and down the stairs, baking cookies that sold almost as fast as I made them. The crowds only grew. Until finally at three pm, we had to cry uncle.

Mom turned the open sign over to closed and we both nearly sagged to the floor.

"I haven't had a day like that since the pumpkin cheese-cakes of 2018."

"It's got to be the movie people. None of those people had proper coats."

Bobby's system for identifying the movie people seemed pretty ironclad.

"Shit," I breathed. "Bobby."

"What's wrong?" Mom asked, picking herself up from the window to come around the counter and start cleaning up.

"Nothing," I said. "We're supposed to go sledding." I said it like he was taking me to the moon and nothing had ever been so ridiculous.

"That sounds fun."

"Does it?" I asked, and headed back into the kitchen just as Bobby was coming in the back door.

"Hey!" he said, and then took in the carnage of the kitchen. "What happened here?"

"We sold out of everything," I said. "We haven't had a day like that in years."

"My parents said the same thing. Dad is going to be roasting coffee all night."

"Proof the movie is good for the town, I guess." I started picking up the dough scoops, the empty dough bins and the dirty cookie trays and putting them in the sink. "Hey, I know we have a date, but I don't think I can..."

Bobby was taking off his coat and rolling up his sleeves.

"What are you doing?"

"Dishes," he said.

"You don't have to do that. Mom and I-"

"Have been on your feet all day. Let me help."

Let me help. Let me help. Let me help.

I was so tired, it was all I could do not to cry.

I grabbed everything around the kitchen and the front of the bakery and set it on the stainless steel table opposite the dish station. It was like an incantation, those words. A spell. Better than bippityboppityboo. Better than I wish upon a star.

Better than anything any man had ever said to me.

I'll believe in the person I love.

"Oh, Bobby," Mom said, coming into the kitchen. "Thank you for helping out."

"My pleasure," he said over his shoulder. "Why don't you two grab the flask in the inside pocket of my coat and have a seat while I finish this up?"

Mom and I looked at each other with a grin and a shrug.

I pulled out the flask he'd slipped in his pocket. Then Mom and I sat on the stainless steel table and passed it back and forth while we told him about our day.

"I think tomorrow we have to double everything," Mom said. "At least until Christmas. Especially the iced cookies."

"Mom, we are out of dough."

"Out of everything?" Mom asked, like she was finally understanding what we were up against.

"Cupboards are bare."

She hung her head and then laughed. "Okay. Well, let's start making dough."

One final swig from the flask for each of us, then we hopped off the table as Bobby put the clear plastic bins upside down on the counter to dry.

"Your date!" Mom cried, looking at Bobby and then back at me. "You should go have fun. I can start..."

"Mom, I'm not leaving you to make all the dough by yourself."

"Yeah, me neither," Bobby said. "Listen, if my dads taught me anything, it's how to brew a perfect cup of coffee, turn the other cheek and follow a recipe."

"Do we even have a recipe?" I asked Mom. We'd been making our cookies for so long it was all memorized.

"Of course," Mom said, and pulled a binder out of the bottom of the old filing cabinet in the corner of the room. I started pulling out the ingredients.

"You don't have to do this," I told him, as we set him up at the stand mixer filled with pounds of butter and sugar.

"I know," he said with a smile. It wasn't an act, this help-fulness.

Mom got out her secret stash of Jameson's and we each had a coffee cup for sipping. "I hope you don't mind, but we have some baking music," Mom said.

"I would be disappointed if you didn't."

"Well, you haven't heard it yet."

"If it's not a Christmas album, I'm going to be really upset."

Mom was wild-eyed with delight and I groaned. "Now you've done it," I said as Mom pressed play on her favorite Christmas album of all time.

"A Charlie Brown Christmas!" Bobby swung my mom into a twirl, then a slow dance, while I smiled and scraped the sides of the mixing bowl.

"Hey," he said, coming back to his station. "That's my job."

We doubled our already doubled batches and baked the first two dozen of each type in the oven in the bakery. Only then did I see Mom's energy start to flag.

"Hey," I said. "I'll clean up, you head on home."

"No, let's get this done," Mom said. "It'll be better if we do it together."

She was right. She was always right. That had been her motto for my brother and me growing up. When we were together, it was better. Always.

Bobby slid right into this mess like he'd been a part of it for years. I understood in part why Mom kept men outside the circle of us, the fear of somehow messing up the chemistry or the balance of what we had. She was the one who taught me balance in relationships. You didn't take more than what you gave. But you also never asked for help when you had nothing left to give. It was a catch-22.

But she shouldn't have been scared. She should have let someone in, if for no other reason than it could have made things even better. Seeing my mom being loved by a man who was worthy of her love might have been worth the risk.

"Hey," Bobby said. "I'm going to give your mom a lift home."

"Really?" I asked. Mom didn't live far, but it was one in the morning and she'd been on her feet for over eighteen hours.

"Really. You okay locking up? I can-"

"Walk me home, too? I'm ten steps away. I'll be fine. Thank you."

He slipped an arm around my waist. "You better tell me quick if this isn't okay, because I'm going to kiss you in front of your mother and the gingerbread dough if you don't-"

I reached up and smacked a kiss on his lips. Loud and messy and mostly joking. He laughed against my mouth and held me close. Settling me down until the joke was gone and all that was left was the kiss.

"You guys get out of here," Mom said, clicking off the lights and grabbing the keys from the hook by the door. "I'll lock up."

"I got it, Mom," I said and took the keys from her. "Bobby's going to give you a ride home."

"Oh...well, I won't turn that down. I'm exhausted." Mom said with a laugh.

We all piled into our coats and stepped out into the cold air, so sharp it made me suck in a breath. It made me feel alive and clear.

"Mom," I said. "You should call Scott, I think. Ask how his latest book is going."

She looked at me, wide-eyed. "Honey, that was ages ago."

"Yes, but he still comes in every Sunday for a reason, and now I don't think it's our scones."

"Ha. Go to bed," she said and kissed my forehead. "Bobby and I will watch and make sure you get up there okay."

Bobby and Mom got into his truck, the lights came on, illuminating the steps as I climbed up to my apartment. I felt their eyes on me, their presence. Instead of making me itchy, or conflicted in any way, I only felt cared for.

My phone buzzed as soon as I got in my door.

> Bobby: I had fun. Thanks. See you tomorrow.

Then another text from Mom:

> Mom: Honey. He's such a keeper.

A keeper, I thought. Only hadn't I promised myself I never wanted to *keep* anyone?

Not even a cat.

Which was maybe why I adopted Fleabag. Because he wasn't really mine, was he?

12

Bobby

At the office, my assistant, Eddie, revealed why there was a sudden surge of new people in town. "Tiktok. He's posting Tiktoks."

"Who is?" I asked, drinking coffee and trying to make sense of what I was looking at on Eddie's phone. There was snow, and Jake Foxhall's handsome/stupid face. Some kind of dance people were doing behind him that he looked too cool to do. Or maybe too embarrassed. "Wait...is that? Those are my parents!" I cried, grabbing his phone. "And Madame Za?"

"Yeah, that's what I'm telling you," Eddie said. As an assistant, Eddie Shah was actually younger than me, but he was the best. Super organized, unlimited amounts of enthusiasm, but he insisted on work/life balance, which meant he walked out the door every day at five and he didn't answer email or non-emergency texts at home.

It took some getting used to, because my job as sheriff felt like more of a twenty four hour a day deal, but we'd figured out how to work with each other.

"The film company is posting tons of TikTok's about the town. I think they're using the setting as a way to increase interest in the movie."

He scrolled through other videos of the beach all covered in ice, but the surfers were out there anyway. The Christmas tree in the square. My parent's coffee shop. The dress shop. Pappas' Diner.

"Well, it's working," I said. You could tell by just looking out the window, the square had tons of foot traffic. Ani's Beach Shop, was now a Christmas shop. The book store was packed and Bobbette and Belle was lined up out the door.

"Well, you've got a ten o'clock with the mayor and then a conference call with the governor."

"The Governor?" Did my voice just break?

"Maybe she's on Tiktok. Maybe we should be on Tiktok?"

"Don't get ahead of yourself, Eddie."

I had plans to take Mari sledding, to make up for missing last night, but the day was a marathon run at a sprinter's pace. Traffic jams. Altercations in lines. All out battles for the last items on the shelves in stores.

Why was everyone so angry? It was Christmas!

It was around four that afternoon when I realized I had to cancel my plans with Mari, so I shot her a quick text asking for a rain check. By eight things were finally starting to wear down, and I had this urge just to hear her voice.

"Hmmm," she said when she answered.

"Shit. Are you sleeping? Did I wake you up?"

"Hmmm," she said.

I imagined her on her couch and wanted to head over

there and slip in behind her. Put my arm around her waist and finish that nap with her.

"Hey, do you need help making more dough?"

"No," she said. "We're okay. Just...all the people. From everywhere. They need sugar. So tired."

I smiled into the phone. "Okay, I'll call you tomorrow."

"Okay."

I hung up and Eddie poked his head in the door. This was a first. "Do you know how late it is? Why are you still here?" I asked him.

"Sometimes the occasion warrants it. Besides, we might have a chance for Calico Cove to go viral."

I shook my head. "I don't even know what that means."

Eddie held up his phone. "Just started our Tiktok account."

"I'm not dancing," I told him.

"Famous last words," Eddie said. "You have a call on line two."

"It's not the President, right?"

"Don't flatter yourself."

I didn't. I just picked up line two. "Sheriff Tanner."

Mari

EVERY DAY we started off with the shelves full of cookies, scones, mini gingerbread cakes, cranberry squares and pumpkin muffins. Every day Mom and I looked at each other and thought – today, they can't clean us out. Today we are over prepared.

Then they cleaned us out.

It was days of this.

The Christmas dates with Bobby had been pushed back by each of us.

"I'm sorry," he said with a giant yawn the other night. There'd been a terrible drunk driving hit and run accident on the highway over in Prescott, and Bobby had been coordinating with emergency crews and the police to find the man who'd fled the scene.

"Don't be sorry, Bobby. You've been working crazy hours."

"We were going sledding, damnit!"

I rolled my eyes. "Sure. One of these days, Bobby. We will go sledding."

On Friday night Bobby came over to my apartment, sled in his truck, but it was freezing rain. We both decided there was no way sledding could be fun in freezing rain, so instead, exhausted by the week, we shared a pizza and a six pack of beer. Together we laid down on my couch and watched his favorite Christmas movie.

"It's like a Christmas date," he said.

"This isn't a Christmas movie," I said, taking the last sip of my beer and setting it on the floor by my couch.

"Bite your tongue, woman."

"They don't say Yipee-ki-yay, Mother Fucker in Christmas movies. It's a rule."

"Come here," he said, pulling me up against his chest. "Hey," he said as he pressed play. "Have you seen these Tiktoks?" he asked.

"Nope."

"Jake Foxhall is doing all of them," he said, and I turned to look at him, something in his tone making me... wary. But he was watching a blonde man shoot up a Christmas party. "I can't believe how much tourism they've brought in. He even got my parents to be in one. It's incredible."

"Yeah," I said, a little bitterly. "That's what he does."

He turned to see me in the light of the movie. Red and green and the Nakatomi Plaza reflected in his eyes. "You okay?"

I wasn't. But I didn't know how to tell him that.

SATURDAY WAS another busy day and we had the Okinde twins come in and help. When Charlie turned the sign to closed we all sagged against whatever was closest to us. For Mom it was me. For Charlie it was the floor.

"What is going on?" Ramona asked.

"It's like this all over town," Mom said. "Every business is absolutely booming."

"It's because of the dancing Tiktoks." Charlie said.

"Tiktoks?" I asked. "Honey, you have to get off the floor."

"But my feet are worn to nothing."

"It only feels that way."

I helped him off the floor and we all sat on the loveseats we had for brides when they came in for cake tastings. "Everyone is talking about these things. Show me."

There were three accounts. Jake's personal account, the movie account and then another one called Holiday romcom magic. All of them focused on the movie and Calico Cove. "Oh my god, are those Bobby's dads?" I asked.

"Are they dancing?" Mom asked. "Why hasn't anyone asked us to dance? I'd dance. I love to dance."

I couldn't help but laugh. My guess was Jake knew exactly how I'd respond to him showing up here and asking me to dance in a video.

"I can't believe how many views these get," Charlie said, scrolling through his sister's phone. The end of day sunlight came in through the window like a laser and highlighted the flour and sugar that was on their skin. They sparkled.

"Well, Bobby was right," I said with a sigh, leaning back against the chair. "That's why it's so packed."

Of course I wanted to be mad at Asshole Jake, but what was good for Calico Cove was good for Bobette and Belle.

"I have to go to that dinner tonight," I moaned. I'd been too busy lately to dread it, but now all that dread landed like a metal ball in my stomach.

"Okay, you go upstairs and change. The twins and I will clean up," Mom said.

"But we don't have feet," they moaned.

"If I order pizza and bubble tea..."

"We have feet!" They cried.

I wanted nothing but to stay and hang out with these people, but there was a party to go to. And I smelled like cake and sweat.

I grabbed my phone and coat on the way out the door and texted Bobby.

> Mari: Should we just meet there?

> Bobby: Heck no. I'll grab you. Should I bring a bottle of wine or something?

> Mari: I have a bottle and I'm bringing desserts.

> Bobby: Okay. I need to shower and I'll be at yours at 7.

> Mari: I have to shower too.

> Bobby: I could come to you and we could do our part for the environment?

> Mari: Conserve water?

> Bobby: Something like that.

Was it wrong that my first instinct was to agree to shower sex with Bobby? I was dreading this party and I wouldn't mind going with a little sex bliss brain fog. Bobby could deliver that and we could show up at this party a team of two, bonded by orgasms.

But it felt like I was using Bobby for courage and that didn't feel right.

Was sex courage even a thing?

> Mari: I'll leave the door open. Meet me in the bathroom.

> Bobby: Are you joking? Because I am not joking.

> Mari: I am not joking

> Bobby: Be there in five.

Yeah, I thought, heading upstairs, this was going to be good.

BOBBY

I BROKE EVERY SPEED LIMIT. Only to arrive at the foot of her stairs and hesitate.

Get a grip, Bobby. Get a fucking grip.

There was a part of my brain trying to remind me this woman was all I'd wanted for a very long time. So the likelihood of me maybe fucking shit up was very high. Even higher was me coming in my pants like a teenager. Even higher was me blurting out I love you the second I got inside of her body.

So, there were several scenarios where things could go wrong and I was the problem in every one of them.

I gave myself a game plan – a list of rules, that basically went as follows:

Keep your mouth shut.

That was it. My whole strategy. It was enough to send me up the stairs. True to her word the door was open, which I should probably give her some shit for, but that was off topic.

I could hear the shower running. Light and steam were coming out from under her bathroom door. She's in there, I thought. Naked and wet and warm....

My coat hit the couch. I toed off my boots and left a trail of my uniform across the floor. I pushed open the door to her bathroom in just my underwear and socks. The socks I got rid of.

"That better be Sheriff Bobby Tanner."

"It is."

She pulled aside the polka dot shower curtain and grinned at me. Her dark hair was piled up on her head and dark curls clung to her neck and her pink shoulders.

"Hi," she said with a smile.

"Hi," I smiled back, and took off my underwear. I was a strong man. Tough. I had restraint and fortitude, but when she looked at me like I was a bowl of cream and she was a cat who really loved cream – it was all I could do to keep my cool.

"You want to come in?" she asked, pulling the curtain open a little wider. I saw the slope of her breast, a pink nipple.

"Yep," I said and pushed the curtain back a little wider. "Jesus, woman," I hissed, jumping to the far end of the tub. "You trying to kill a man?"

"Too hot?"

"You could say that."

She turned and bent to adjust the temperature, and I would have happily been scalded alive for that view. I ran my hand down her spine. To her hips. Her skin, slippery and warm. She was a perfect hourglass.

You are perfect.

I kept the words behind my teeth and slipped my hands around her waist, cupping her breasts. The water falling down on both of us. I walked her backwards so the water wouldn't hit her face or her hair and I pulled her in as tight as I could. Her round ass against my cock. Her head at my shoulders. I worried about being too far gone. About being so mad for her I'd make a fool of myself, but when she turned and looked up at me, her face was flush with desire. Her eyes liquid with it.

I remembered in a way that made my dick twitch against her ass the way this woman liked to be talked to during sex. I let go of Bobby Tanner, love sick fool, and became Bobby Tanner, caveman.

"How long have you been waiting for me in this shower?" I asked her, sucking water off her shoulder in sips.

"A while."

"You been thinking about me, in this shower? About what I'm going to do to you?"

She nodded.

"You been making yourself wet for me?" I asked. Again she nodded. "Show me."

The breath she took filled up her whole body. It lifted her rib cage into my arms. She took one of my hands and slipped it over her stomach, sluicing water off her skin down to her pussy. Where she stopped.

"Mari," I said, and she pushed my hand further, until my long middle finger slipped through her folds over her clitoris. We both groaned and I circled the rough pad of my finger over her clit again. And then again. Until her whole body twitched and she put her hand out against the tile wall like the earth was falling away.

"I want you to come like this," I said in her ear, licking her ear lobe and then taking it between my teeth. "On my finger. I want you to make yourself come."

I held my finger still against her clit, applying pressure while she slowly rocked her hips against me.

"Yes," she breathed. "Harder."

I gave her more pressure. Another finger. She put her foot up on the lip of the tub, rocking her hips.

"Good?"

"Yes."

"Tell me."

"I love the way you touch me," she said. "I love the way you talk to me. This is the best fucking thing..." her breath started breaking and all my willpower crumbled.

I love you. I love fucking you. I love the way you feel and the way you make me feel. I can hardly believe who I am with you and I want to spend the rest of my life making you come.

"Bobby," she moaned, the tremors starting in her legs. Her hips. Her whole body was shaking. She gripped my hand so hard she might have broken a finger. I might have come against the crack of her ass...okay I did do that, because why not come with her?

The world might have fallen off its axis. I didn't know. I was barely in my body.

She turned in my arms, her eyes limpid with...everything.

"Come on," she said, and cranked off the water.

She pushed aside the shower curtain and tossed me a towel. Then she reached to grab her own and the way her body moved...my dick was hard again in a heartbeat.

The desire was a fever. A blindness. Who the fuck needed to dry off? I stepped out of the shower, put my arm around her waist, lifted her off her feet and carried her from the bathroom to her bedroom. She laughed the whole way, shrieking to be let down, but I ignored her. This was some caveman shit.

I threw her on the bed, where she bounced once and then sprawled under me as I prowled up her body.

"What's gotten into you?" she asked.

"You."

I paused at her pussy, pink and ripe, she smelled like soap and her orgasm. I spread her legs out wide and licked her taste into my mouth.

"Bobby," she sighed, her fingers feathering through my hair, soft sweet touches that were a side of this woman I could not get enough of. "Do you have a condom?" she asked.

"Yep," I said. I'd gotten cocky maybe, but I couldn't bare the idea that I wouldn't be prepared for this exact moment. "In my pants."

"Where are they?"

"Hallway."

"That's too far."

She fumbled at her bedside table and started pulling things out. A bunch of books. Hand cream.

A vibrator.

"Hold on a second," I said, and leaned down to pick it up where she'd tossed it on the rug.

"Later, buddy. Later we get fancy. Right now I just...." She sat up and opened the condom with her teeth which was the most feral, sexy thing I'd ever seen. My cock, knowing what was coming, was leaking pre-come everywhere like I didn't come five minutes ago.

She slipped the condom over my dick and I hissed at the pleasure. Every muscle straining to her. For her.

"Come on, Bobby," she whispered, and tugged me down into the sweet spot between her parted thighs.

"I'm..." I stopped. My face in her neck.

"You're what?" she breathed as I reached down, notching myself against her, the head of my cock bathed in her heat and wet. I couldn't breathe for the pleasure of it. The near pain of it. How perfect she was.

In love.

"Crazy for you," I said. It was the closest I could get to the truth. Then I sank deep inside of her. One thrust and it felt like I'd never been so deep inside a woman.

We both moaned. Her legs came up around my waist and I braced my knees against her mattress.

"Are you okay?" I asked, my face still buried in her neck. "This... I can't..."

"Go," she said, urging me on. "Just go..."

I did. Fucking her like it was the last thing I was going to do on this earth and I needed to do it right. Deep long thrusts, quick short bursts. All of it. Every possible way until she was panting and bucking up to meet me.

I reached down between our slick bodies, my thumb finding her clit and pressing against it until I felt the tension in her body change. Coil.

"Fuck, yes," I breathed. "Come on. Let go."

Four hard thrusts and she shattered against me and I let go of everything. Of any bit of restraint I had left. Every wall came down and I held onto her as tight as I could, coming so hard the world was different.

I was different.

Still I kept the words behind my teeth. Deep in my throat. I found the strength to lift my head and our eyes met. She smiled, sweet and satisfied, all woman.

My woman.

I broke apart like a cheap pinata.

"I love you."

13

Bobby

I had a list of shit I'd messed up in my life. Not a huge list, but a regular sized one. I got fired from my first part-time job for being an idiot. I lied to my dads about taking the car after curfew and got caught. I failed high school math. Twice.

But this sudden icy distance between me and Mari, felt like an epic fail. Like a life-changing one.

I'd told her I loved her. She'd said nothing. So I'd told her I had to take care of the condom.

Romantic stuff.

Now we were sitting in the truck getting ready to go to this stupid party and I couldn't take her silence anymore.

"Look, can you just forget I said anything?" I said.

"Bobby, please stop freaking out about it."

"It just... it just slipped out."

"So, you didn't mean it?" she asked me, her eyes shining in the dark.

I had no idea what was the right answer. Did she want me to have been drunk on sex and the words just slipped out? Would that make her feel better? It would make me feel like shit. I wasn't going to lie to her. Not about this.

"No," I said. "I meant it. I didn't just have a crush on you, Mari."

She turned back towards the passenger side window, her face hidden by her hair.

"I just didn't mean to say it so soon," I told her. "I was going to wait until I knew how you felt."

"I told you what to expect from me," she said, her voice low. "I told you I didn't want the fairy tale, because I don't believe in it."

"I know. But..."

"You were just going to wear me down?"

She smiled as she said it, and it felt like a tiny thaw in the chill between us. But I didn't know if it was real or because I wanted it so badly.

"Something like that," I confessed, and she took a deep breath.

Then the silence returned. I'd said my piece and knew there was no convincing her with words. She was the only person who could change her mind. It was one of the things I liked so much about her. The way she knew herself. Mari was unmoved by outside forces.

We drove that way, in chilly silence for a while, and I forced myself to be okay with it. To just sit with it. With her. Trying, as best I could, to give her time.

"Where is this house?" she finally asked after we passed Hanolan's Pointe.

"It's Declan's old house." Declan, the class trouble

maker, was also a brilliant architect. No one saw that coming in high school.

"No shit," she said.

"Yeah, the one he built but never lived in."

We climbed the gravel road up the cliffside to the top. There was a glass and stone house that somehow managed to look modern and like it was built out of the mountain all at the same time. Rumor was, Declan designed it before leaving town in the middle of the night without any explanation.

I pulled my truck up behind a Tesla and a Mercedes S series and what I thought might be a Bentley. But I also recognized Ani Wong's Subaru and Fiona's old Jaguar from her modeling days. Matthew Sullivan's truck was there too.

"Is Carrie going to be here?" I asked.

"Probably, why?"

"Matt Sullivan is here," I said.

"Uh oh, when was the last time they were in the same room?"

"Had to be that high school reunion when she threw the drink in his face and he called her a stuck-up snob?"

"Well, I guess the entertainment portion of the night is sorted," Mari said, with all the excitement of someone going to the dentist.

"We don't have to go," I said. She hadn't disclosed any more of what happened between her and Jake, but I was still #teamMari all the way and if she wanted to leave, we would leave.

"No," she said, resigned. "The food is probably going to be amazing."

"Well, we know the desserts will be," I said, and grabbed the Bobbette And Belle box and the silver bowl of whipped cream on the seat between us. I popped the truck door and was about to get out when I felt Mari's hand on mine.

"I'm sorry, Bobby." she said.

"For what?"

"For handling all of that wrong. Earlier. Everything... you said."

Something sunk in me. She couldn't even say the word love, even in a secondhand way.

"It's all right," I said.

"You're not a very good liar, Bobby."

I turned my hand around so I could hold hers.

"Hey, I don't need you to love me back right now. I get it. From where you're standing, this all happened really fast. But I've been loving you for years, so nothing has really changed except now you know it. So you don't need to be sorry, you just need... to not be weird about it."

"You know it is impossible for me *not* to be weird, right?"

"Come on, let's get in there and show asshole Jake that you've moved on and eat his food."

She sighed heavily and I realized, she was actually... nervous. More than nervous, maybe.

"Do you want to tell me what happened between you two?"

"No, I mean, yes. I will. But not now. You're right. Let's go in there and demolish what will probably be a very excellent cheese course."

"That's the spirit."

The house was out of a movie. Lit up perfectly so that every single room and every single person in the room seemed to glow. There were elegant Christmas trees in every corner and it was packed with gorgeous people.

I glanced down at Mari, and yep, she glowed too.

A man came and took our gifts. Another man collected

Mari's bakery box, the silver bowl of whipped cream and whisked it away. Someone else came by with trays of champagne with pomegranate seeds in the bottom. Mari, I noticed, downed hers like a shot. I handed her mine and she did the same.

"All right?" I asked.

"Better."

"When should I start worshipping you?" I asked her.

"Huh?" Her eyes got wide and I could tell she was getting even more freaked out by the second.

"Remember, that was the point of all of this," I said.

"Oh. Yeah. Now is good."

"Do I just trust my gut, or is there some kind of threshold you would like?"

"Just touch me. A lot. Like, I guess, you have been. Also laugh at my jokes."

"You tell jokes?"

She punched my shoulder and I slipped my arm around her waist, ready and willing to play the worshipping fiancé all night long if it was required.

"The sheriff and the baker!" A voice shouted as we walked into the room.

Jake Foxhall, wearing a black turtleneck that should have looked stupid but made him look like a superhero in disguise, left a group of people and came over to say hello. The conversation he'd been a part of stopped when he left and everyone turned to watch him greet us.

"I'm so glad you could make it," Jake said, kissing Mari's cheek. He half shook my hand, half hugged me at the same time like people did on TV, but I never really thought they did in real life.

"We brought dessert but someone took it at the door."

"Of course," Jake said, waving his hand. "The staff will take care of that. Can I introduce you around?"

I glanced around and saw Fiona, Ani and Matt Sullivan on the far edge of a group of people. Ani wore her bright red glasses that looked so sharp against her silver hair. Fiona looked like a million dollars in a green velvet dress that managed to cover her completely and somehow make her look like the sexiest woman in the room. Sullivan, painfully underdressed in jeans and flannel shirt, was pretending to ignore Carrie Piedmont on the other side of the room.

But we were being pulled by Jake to a group of strangers.

"Everyone, this is Bobby, the local sheriff, and this is Mari, the artist from college I told you all about."

Mari went absolutely still under my arm like she'd been electrocuted.

"What did you tell them?" she asked, through lips that barely moved.

"What do you mean? I told them you were the most talented person I knew at school." Jake said, like he was impervious to Mari's vibe.

She looked up at me with a fake smile on her face, but absolute rage in her eyes. My arm went slack around her waist. I wasn't sure what the fuck was going on. I should have insisted she tell me the history between her and Jake so I knew how to act right now.

"Were you an actress too?" one of the women in the group asked her.

"No. I was a painter."

"A painter. Do you still paint?"

"No." Mari said with such finality, the woman looked embarrassed.

"So your dads run the coffee shop, right?" Jake asked me, stepping smoothly into the awkwardness.

"Yeah. Ed and Bruce. You somehow managed to get them to do a dance on video."

"They were fantastic. Really good sports," Jake said. There was a brief conversation among the movie people about plans for other social media opportunities around town.

"This is so typical." Mari said to Jake, her voice slicing through the happy chatter.

"What's that, love?" Jake asked, his pleasant smile still on his face.

A server came by with a tray full of drinks and I grabbed two, trying to press one into Mari's hands. She took it but didn't drink.

Jake took a sip of his and then shrugged. "I'm just trying to help out the town. It's good for the people here. I've noticed your bakery has been packed every day."

"They've had to triple the dough for the cookies," I said with a smile, wanting to change the strange chemistry in this room right now.

"Our bakery was doing just fine before you showed up," Mari said with narrowed eyes.

"Yes, and now it's doing better," Jake said with a smile. "I'm doing you a favor, Mari."

"I remember your favors, *Jake*. And they come at a cost."

"Mari," Fiona was suddenly standing on Mari's other side. With incredible social grace that I guess I just wasn't capable of, she pulled her into a smaller conversation, taking the tension in the room down by half. Jake turned away, but before he did I caught his eye.

He lifted his eyebrows in a way that could only mean, "good luck with her."

Stunned, and thinking maybe I read it wrong, I turned

away too and found Sullivan and Ani standing by the book shelves, sharing a plate of appetizers.

"Have you had the lobster tortellini?" Ani asked, lifting a wide spoon with a tiny piece of pasta on it, artfully decorated with tiny herbs and flakes of sea salt.

"I have not," I said. Ani, with speed and deftness, slipped one into my mouth.

"So good," Ani said.

I nodded.

"Not as good as the beef stuff," Sullivan said.

"What beef stuff?" I asked, putting my hand over my mouth.

"I don't know. It had beef and it had bread. Also some sauce."

"Where is it?"

"In his stomach," Ani said, poking Sullivan in the side.

"Yeah, sorry, mate. They were just too good."

"Why does Mari have that look on her face any time she talks to Jake?" Ani asked.

"What look?"

"Like she's looking for a knife and a shallow grave."

"They knew each other in college and Mari isn't his biggest fan," I said. I looked across the room at her where she was standing with Carrie and Fiona. The tension wasn't at all gone from her body. She radiated tension.

"Not the biggest fan of Jake Foxhall?" Ani asked.

"No," I said, wishing I knew what was upsetting her so much.

"And what about you?" Ani asked Sullivan.

"What about me?"

"You're standing in the same room as Carrie Piedmont and so far no one is bleeding."

"That was childhood shit. I've moved on."

"Why do I doubt that?" I snorted.

"Fine. I've moved on if she stays on her side of the room."

"Ask one of the locals!" Jake cried, and the small clutch of movie people turned our way. It was intimidating being the focus of all that star power. Their teeth alone were blinding.

"Ask us what?" Ani prompted.

"What's the deal with all the cats around town?" One of the men who worked in the production staff asked.

Our small group was absorbed by the movie crowd, and Ani told an attentive audience all about the pirates fleeing a burning ship, swimming to shore with cats inside of their hats. I searched for Mari in the crowd. But couldn't find her.

Mari

YOU KNOW that feeling when you're in a movie theater and something is funny, like really funny – but somehow, you're the only one who laughs? It's embarrassing, sure, but at the same time you're looking around at the other people like... what is wrong with you, that you didn't find that funny?

That was me at this party.

Except nothing was funny and I was the only one who saw Jake Foxhall for who he really was.

I walked down the hallway that led to the kitchen, where I did not want to go as it was absolutely filled with catering staff who would immediately ply me with food my stomach was too upset to eat.

The first door I tried was a small dark study with a desk

and more floor to ceiling windows looking out onto the dark ocean. The lighthouse was the only bright spot in a landscape of midnight blue.

Was I the only one who felt the malice rolling off of Jake? Was I the only one who felt like we were toys, and he was a kid determined to play with us so hard we broke?

Maybe what hurt more was Bobby's obvious discomfort with my discomfort.

What can you possibly expect from the guy? I thought. He told you he loved you and you said, nothing. Like an asshole.

"Mari?"

The last person I expected to follow me was Carrie. Even though she was local, I was still starstruck.

"Hi," I said, trying to gather myself into some semblance of a grown up and not a teenager being fucked around by the hottest guy in theater school. "Sorry, I was just getting a minute of quiet."

"I understand," she said graciously, but stepped further into the room.

She wore a pair of wide legged black pants and a cream silk blouse that made her deep red hair look like a color in a Botticelli painting. I felt extremely shabby in my black leggings and long blue blazer. "Do you mind if I join you, for just a second?"

"Sure," I said, surprised she wanted to talk to me. Carrie was three years ahead of me in school and so clearly bound for greatness that our paths had never really crossed. "It must be so strange to be back here."

"It's lovely to be back here," she said. "I wish I'd been able to come back more often. I've missed Calico Cove. A lot."

"Well, it's not Hollywood, but it has its charms."

"It's paradise compared to Hollywood." She looked out over the ocean and the lighthouse. The glow of Piedmont Island just past the headlands.

"How is your mom?" I asked. There'd been rumors in Calico Cove that she'd been sick. Matthew, who ran the ferry out to the island, said she was practically on death's door.

Carrie laughed. "Mom is going to outlive all of us. I think she invents illnesses to try and get me home."

"How about your grandmother?"

"Granny's half-pickled in rum and believes she's currently being kept alive by a Greek tarot card reader."

"Oh no, how does Madame Za feel about that?"

"I'm not sure she knows."

Oh, I thought. She knows.

Carrie turned to me, her cream blouse gleaming like vanilla ice cream. "As much as I could talk about my family all night, that's not why I wanted to talk to you."

There was the bang of a pan being dropped in the kitchen and the sound of feet hustling down the hallway. Someone was getting reprimanded in the kitchen.

"I swear to God, he keeps this house so tense," she said. "Like the air conditioner is cranked too high. Look, I know we didn't know each other in school so you might not have much reason to trust me, but Jake alluded to your past and I can see you're obviously not buying his bullshit, so I thought we should talk," Carrie said. "I'm trying to get Jake off this movie."

"What? Why?"

"Because he's a vindictive asshole who isn't happy unless he's got a woman tied up in knots. He has this nasty little habit of getting revenge on anyone who tells him no, or more importantly, steals the spotlight away from him."

"You?"

"No, he doesn't pull his shit with me," she said, and I realized she would be far too powerful for his games. "Though the fact that Matt fucking Sullivan somehow got on the guest list indicates Jake's *trying* to mess with me. I need someone not part of the movie set who can talk to the producers about his behavior. If you have a past with him, you must know how he is."

"Oh, yeah. I know how he is."

I realized what an opportunity I was being given. To not just tell my side of the story, no matter how unbelievable it might seem, but to punish Jake for some of what he put me through.

He'd taken away school, my dreams as an artist. My confidence as a woman. And yes, I was fine now. Better, for having come home. Working with my mom. Being among friends.

Bobby.

There was a wild surge in my chest.

I was better for having found my way back to Bobby.

However, if Jake was still up to his game, he needed to be called out for that shit.

"I would love to make a statement if you think it will help."

"I do," she said. "Can I call you after Christmas?"

"I look forward to it."

"Good. Now I'll let you get back to your doting fiancé," Carrie said, her green eyes twinkling at me in the half-dark.

Right. My fiancé. Who didn't even understand why I was acting so weird.

Who'd told me he loved me after making me come so hard I pulled a muscle, and I'd said nothing. Ugh.

I needed to find Bobby and try to make things right. To

explain that I did need to go slow, but that I was happy he loved me. I felt better and fuller – because he loved me.

Carrie opened the door of the study just then into the bright and busy hallway, only to nearly hit the devil himself. Jake Foxhall.

That turtleneck looks stupid.

"There you are, Carrie," he said. He was smiling, but his eyes were sharp and calculating, shifting from Carrie to me and back. "We're sitting down for dinner."

"Wonderful," Carrie said with the least convincing smile I'd ever seen, and put her arm around me and steered me back towards the party.

"Mari, can I talk to you for a second in the kitchen?" he asked, trying to sound casual but not completely hitting the mark.

"Sorry," I said, over my shoulder. "Dinner is waiting for us."

14

Bobby

The dining room had been set with a long table, with candlesticks and pine boughs down the center. Each table setting looked like a little work of art, with ivory dishes and bright red napkins. It was all wasted on me.

When Mari walked in I finally sat down, not relaxed, but at least able to breathe again. Something serious was going on and I was on the outside of it. I hated that.

"Hi," I said, as she came to her spot next to mine.

"Hi," she said, and then to my surprise, and, not going to lie – delight and relief, she cupped my face in her hands and kissed me. She kissed me until Ani whistled and someone else started clapping.

She leaned back with a smile.

"Are we at the worshipping me part of the night?" I whispered.

"I'm sorry," she whispered back.

"Nothing to apologize for."

I stood and pulled out her chair. I accidentally caught Jake's eye as I sat, and he was watching Mari with something that could only be called calculation on his face. However, when I caught his eye, he gave me his wide movie star smile.

Across from me Carrie was watching the whole thing with a smile on her face. She winked at me, and then before Jake could start a conversation about what he wanted to do for the town, she started asking people around the table about their favorite Christmas memories.

Soon everyone was laughing and talking and the wine was flowing. Mari, beside me, relaxed and sipped her white wine.

"The rule at my house on Christmas morning was, we couldn't go downstairs until everyone was ready," I said, when it came around to my turn. Plates were being set down in front of us. Salads with ribbons of cucumbers and edamame and tiny little lettuces. "So Pop and I would sit on the steps, while Dad absolutely took his time getting ready. He'd shave and shower and ask us which socks he should wear. It was torture. But also kind of fun."

"Delayed gratification," Carrie said with a smile. "What about you, Mari?"

Mari wiped her mouth and put her napkin back in her lap.

"One year my brother and I snuck downstairs and opened all of our presents, and then rewrapped them so our mom wouldn't know what we'd done. Except, we didn't realize she had this wrapping paper code and we ended up putting all the wrong paper on the wrong toys."

"The opposite of delayed gratification," I said.

"Was she mad?" Carrie asked.

"Mom never got mad. She thought we were the cleverest children ever born."

"That's sweet," Jake said, and I was realizing now, what it was about that guy. How his words and his tone never really matched. He could say something nice and make it sound like an insult, or insult someone and make it sound like a compliment.

It was like he wanted everyone to be a little on edge around him. Classic narcissist.

"What about you?" I asked Jake. "Favorite Christmas memories?"

"Tonight," he said, his arms spread wide like he was St. Fucking Nick or whatever. "Good food, good people, a good project on the horizon. It's all good."

There were raised glasses and here heres and then everyone dug into their dinner. Sullivan, across the table, rolled his eyes at me, and I grinned.

Dinner was pretty fucking delicious and on the other side of Mari was Priya, the assistant social media manager, who, come to find out, had been doing all those awesome videos.

"It's not a big deal," she said, tucking her jet black hair behind her ear and casting rather furtive glances over at Jake. "It's literally my job, and Jake is the real star power, people watch just to see him."

"Yes, but they're your ideas," Mari said, rather fiercely. "And they're good. Don't give away the credit."

"I'm not," Priya said. "I just have an excellent team."

"Let's have dessert in the living room," Jake said, pushing away from the table. "Mari, the kitchen staff have asked for your help with the cake."

Mari stood up and I grabbed her hand before she walked away. "Do you need help?"

"I have been cutting cake for a long time," she said, and kissed me on the forehead.

She went down the hallway to the kitchen while the rest of us went in the opposite direction towards the living room, which now had a roaring fire in the fireplace and servers were handing out after dinner cocktails.

"No thank you," I said to a server, trying to hand me a snifter of something. "I'm driving."

Sullivan took my snifter, twirled it, then put his nose inside the glass rim and took a big loud sniff.

"Really?" I asked.

"Pretty sure it's what you're supposed to do." He downed it in one shot. "Holy shit, it burns."

"Classy as ever, Sullivan," Carrie said as she walked by, but did not stop.

Sullivan watched her go, eyes narrowed.

Ani came up to us with her own snifter, hers was full of a creamy booze and ice cubes. "I've never been to such a fancy party," she said.

"Do you love it?" Sullivan asked.

Ani looked around and shrugged. "Meh."

For some reason this struck me as hilarious. I looked around for Mari, who would share the sentiment, but she still wasn't back from the kitchen. I realized then, Jake was absent too.

The hair stood up on the back of my neck.

Enough of this being patient bullshit.

"I'll be right back," I told my friends, and went to find Mari.

Mari

. . .

THE KITCHEN WAS EMPTY. My simple but elegant spice cake already on a cutting board with a stack of plates beside it.

"Hello?" I said into the quiet kitchen, but no one answered. "Weird."

Whatever. I could slice cake. I also brought some whipped cream from the bakery which I assumed was in the fridge. Only, I couldn't easily find the fridge. What, I wondered, was the point of a fridge that looked just like cabinets?

After opening a pantry twice, and a cupboard full of platters, I finally opened the right door. I pulled out my silver bowl of whipped cream and when I shut the door, came face to face with Jake.

"Holy s—-!" I cried, and nearly dropped my bowl. "Oh my god, Jake. You scared me."

"Sorry," he said. His lips were smiling but his eyes were dead. "Are you having a good time?"

"Lovely," I said, and walked around him to the marble island and my cake. "Thank you for inviting us."

"Yes, you and the sheriff are a very cute couple."

I said nothing.

"What were you and Carrie talking about?" Jake asked, standing far too close to me for comfort. I picked up the giant cake cutting knife that had been left beside the cake.

"Nothing really," I said. "Just catching up."

"Why are you lying?" he muttered, practically in my ear. I dropped the knife and stepped back, but he grabbed my wrist. Hard.

"Let go of me," I said through numb lips. I felt this kind of billowing rage, all the times he pulled his insidious shit and made me doubt myself. The way he changed my life and how furious I had been, and unable to deal with it. The way he preyed on me and turned me on myself.

"Not until you tell me-"

"Get your hands off of her," Bobby said, standing in the doorway, looking like a big blonde hero. Jake didn't respond immediately, and I could tell he was furious with Bobby for interrupting. Bobby took another step inside, his eyebrows raised. "I'm not kidding, asshole. Get your hands off her."

Jake stepped back, hands up, smile in place. "Just having a conversation about old times, Bobby. No need to be jealous."

"I'm not jealous. She asked you to get your hands off of her and you didn't. I'm furious." Bobby looked at me. "You okay?"

"Fine."

"Want to get the fuck out of here?"

"Just...just a second," I said, and I picked up my knife and turned to Jake, whose smile faltered.

"No need to get dramatic," he said in his smarmy tone. He lifted his hands like I was going to stab him. "We're all friends here."

"But we're not," I said. "You were never my friend. You were a small man who took advantage of a girl's insecurities because you liked pulling my strings. When I finally caught on to all of it and dumped your ass, you got your revenge."

"This is nonsense," Jake said, and stepped for the door like he wanted to leave, but there was Bobby, standing in his way.

"I don't think she's done," Bobby said. I wasn't sure if he was flexing under his blue shirt, but he looked so big and strong, he made Jake look like a teenage boy.

I sliced the cake into perfectly sized pieces and laid them on the plates.

"He used to tell me that I was lucky he was interested in me. Because I wasn't very pretty and guys didn't like nerdy girls. Yes, I was lucky he found me interesting because no other man would. I was lucky he found me sexy or smart or funny because no other man would. *Lucky. Lucky. Lucky.*" I said with each cut of the knife.

"Jesus," Bobby said.

"I thought we were dating, but no, I was just a booty call. I don't think I was even your first choice booty call. I had to be like third on the list. I was just the booty call he wanted to make cry before he asked for a blow job."

"Mother fucker," Bobby said.

"But that wasn't the worst part, was it Jake? Oh no. The worst part was when I figured out you were a sick fuck, who liked to get in my head, and I tried to dump your ass. We could still be friends, you said. We could support each other's career. You were such a help putting together my first big art showing in New York. You knew all the right people, didn't you? How amazing it was going to be for me."

Jake sighed heavily. "Mari, this is ancient history."

I turned to look at Bobby. "He invited people to the art show who he knew would rip me apart. The most ruthless art critics and patrons in the city, it felt like. I stood in a room filled with my art and listened while people sometimes quietly, and sometimes not so quietly, ripped my work to shreds."

"Mari," Bobby whispered.

"I was cliché. I was a pretender. I was cute. God. That word. I heard that word so much that night. To call me an artist was a joke. That's what they said. And that was all you, Jake. Your people. Your crowd. You put me in that situation just to watch it happen."

"I was trying to show you...you weren't ready for real criticism," Jake shrugged. "I did you a favor."

I nodded. "Yeah, you did. I wasn't good enough for that

crowd, but that was something I needed to learn on my own. Instead, I was nothing more than a bug you felt you needed to squash. Well, now it's my turn."

"What's that supposed to mean?" Jake asked.

"I talked to Priya. Your social media coordinator. Those videos that are so great for the town? All her idea. All her work. But I bet that's not sitting well with you. Her success. What are your plans for her, Jake?"

"You don't know what you're talking about," he said.

"I think I do," I said, and licked some of the whipped cream off my finger. "I think I know all about you. And you won't get away with it, Jake. I won't let you this time."

"What kind of power do you think you have over me?" Jake asked.

"Plenty," I said. "Because I'm not a scared kid anymore. I've got friends. Powerful friends. And I'm engaged to the sheriff, or did you miss that?"

Jake had the sense to look slightly ill.

I sighed and looked at Bobby. "Let's go," I said. "This party sucks."

"Sure," Bobby said without hesitation. "Before we go, do you want me to hold this asshole while you punch him? I'd do the punching for you, but I'm a feminist."

I laughed, which is what he wanted, and I picked up my bowl and walked over to put my arm around Bobby. I regarded Jake the way he used to look at me, like he was just so sad. And I pitied him.

"Goodbye Asshole Jake, I will enjoy watching you crash and burn on social media." I waggled my fingers at him and Bobby put his hand against the small of my back and stepped in behind me.

"You okay?" he asked, as we made our way to the door. Magically, staff was there with our coats.

"I think we're being kicked out."

"You are," Jake said, coming up behind us. He was smiling, but not with his eyes. "Sorry you can't stay for dessert," he said, loud enough that the people in the other room could hear him.

"One second," I said, and stepped into the living room. Jake moved as if to stop me but Bobby got there first.

"Please," he said. "Please give me a reason to break your arm in front of all these people." Jake went pale and sweaty and I couldn't lie. The caveman routine was pretty hot.

Priya and Carrie were talking in the corner, Priya looking slightly tortured, aware undoubtedly that Jake's mood was bad, and that it would somehow be her job to make it better. And I remembered that poisonous feeling all too well. "Priya," I said. "I don't know what happened between you two. But Jake is a manipulative gaslighting abuser."

"It's not... he's just a difficult actor," Priya said, trying, like I had, to make his behavior okay.

"But he's not," Carrie said. "We've worked with difficult actors before and this is targeted abuse."

Priya looked like she might cry. I squeezed her hand.

"I let him ruin my dream," I said. "I let him make me feel like I didn't deserve all the things I wanted." I looked over my shoulder at Bobby. "Don't make the mistakes I did. Carrie, you can reach me at the bakery, anytime."

"Thanks, Mari. I'm really proud of you."

"Well, I'm years too late to help myself, but if I can help anyone else, I'm glad."

I turned and Bobby had our coats by the door.

He was staring down Jake who was across the room from both of us, smiling and laughing like everything was fine.

Bobby, I thought. What were the chances that it was Bobby all along?

I didn't say anything to him. I just wrapped my arms around him and squeezed.

"You ready to get out of here?" he asked me. When he looked at me, when he really looked at me – like no one else was in the room – I felt seen. All the way down to my mistakes and my fear. Down to the person I'd been before Jake ever made me doubt myself, and to the person I was going to be with the shadow of Jake removed.

"So ready," I said.

OUTSIDE THE AIR was sharp enough to hurt my lungs, but I breathed in deep. Deeper maybe than I had in years. I couldn't believe how much I'd let what Jake did to me, change me. He made me small and I'd never been small.

Bobby opened my door for me and then hopped in and started the cold truck. He cranked the heater and we sat there for a second, the moon hanging huge and bright just over the water.

"I'm sorry I didn't tell you," I said to him

"It's your story to tell. You get to pick who you tell it to."

"I've never told anyone... not even my mom."

"Why?"

"It would upset her. And it would embarrass me."

The moonlight cast the truck in shades of grey. Even his electric blue eyes were different. "What changed your mind?" he asked.

"Well, that turtleneck for one-"

"Right?" He asked and put the truck in drive. "What an asshole."

"He's doing what he did to me to Priya. And he's probably done it to dozens of women. Carrie is trying to get him out of the movie and I want him out of this town."

"Amen," he said, and drove us slowly down the snowy mountain road towards the highway. "Hey," he said, glancing over at me. "I'm sorry for how I acted."

"When you offered to hold him while I punched him? No apology necessary."

"No," he laughed.

"When you said you'd break his hand if he touched me?"

"It was his arm, and you liked that?"

"I think I have a secret caveman kink."

"Oh," he laughed. "I know you do. But I'm sorry for getting suckered, for even a second, by his act."

"It's all right. He's had a long time to perfect it."

Bobby stopped at the stop sign. Big snowflakes falling down in the headlights.

"Do you think less of me?" I asked.

"For what?" His gaze was sharp.

"For getting suckered by him in the first place." He put the truck in park and cupped my face in his hands.

"You were manipulated and abused. The only thing I feel is proud of you for how you stood up to him tonight. How you're standing up for Calico Cove. You're amazing. You've always been amazing."

"Since high school?" I said with a smile, warmth spreading through me.

"Since show and tell in kindergarten and you brought in that dead frog."

Behind us a car honked and we both looked to see Matthew Sullivan giving us the finger. He must have left just after us. Bobby put the truck in gear and turned left towards town, and Matthew turned right towards his house.

He pulled up beside my steps and put the truck in park

but didn't turn it off. The way he rubbed his hand over his face made me suddenly nervous.

"I think you have to go back to New York," he said.

"What?"

"Yeah. I think that asshole stole your dream and you need to go get it back."

"Bobby," I laughed, but when he turned to look at me he wasn't joking.

"Art wasn't just something you loved or were good at. It was your whole identity," he said. "It was all you ever wanted to do."

"People change."

"This wasn't change, Mari," He said. "That asshole took it away from you and you came back to Calico Cove to lick your wounds, but you aren't meant for this place. You were never meant for this place."

"But, I'm happy here," I said. "I'm happy with you."

His smile was sad. "But you were meant for more, weren't you? You wanted more and that guy took it away from you, and I'm not going to be the next guy who takes you away from it."

"No, listen to me Bobby." I unbuckled my seatbelt and scooched across the bench seat until I was practically in his lap. "I miss art. I'm mad that he took that away from me. But I love this town. I love my life here. I love you." The words came out without thought, and they weren't a lie. But I hadn't had time to think about it. To fully absorb it. To make the words feel like my truth.

He flinched, and when I tried to touch him he grabbed my hands and held onto them, so tight. He closed his eyes and kissed my fingers. "Good night, Mari."

The way he said it sounded like goodbye. "No. Come upstairs. Let's talk... let's..."

"I think I need to think for a little bit," he said. "I've dreamt of you telling me you loved me for half my life and I never imagined I would feel like... second place."

"Bobby, no, no. I promise. You could never be second place. You could never..." but he wasn't hearing me and the tears fell from my eyes over my lips, filling my mouth with salt and bitter regret. I never wanted to hurt him. Never. But all I was doing was hurting him.

"I think we can probably quit the fake engagement stuff," he said. "You've managed to defeat your nemesis all on your own, without my help."

"What about dinner with your parents tomorrow?"

"Don't come," he said. "It would.... they would just be so excited and I can't stand to break their hearts."

"I love you, Bobby," I said, because it didn't feel like there was anything else I could say.

"Please go," he said, and I realized his eyes were full of tears he was too strong to let fall. "Please," he said. "You're only making this harder."

"Are you breaking up with me?"

"Come on, Mari. We were never really together, were we?"

15

Mari

Bobby drove away and I stood in the cold and watched his taillights vanish in the snow.

Is this a broken heart? It felt awful. It felt like I was being pulled apart in a horrible way and I'd done it to myself.

Still standing in the snow, I called Lola.

"Mari?" she asked, out of breath. "Are you okay?"

"How did you know you loved Jackson?"

"What... ummm...." She trailed off.

I looked at my watch. It wasn't that late, why did she sound so... oh shit.

"Sorry," I said. "Go back to whatever...you were doing."

I hung up and called Vanessa.

"Hey honey," she said.

"Can I ask you a question?"

"Of course," she said.

"How did you know you loved Roy?"

"Oh my gosh, that's a good one. It kind of snuck up on

me, you know? Like I just loved him all along. Not at first sight, because he was so mean, at first. But over time, it was just kind of there."

"Yeah, but how did you *know*?"

"What is going on with you? Do you need me to come over there?"

"No." In fact, I started walking the opposite way. Across the road to my mom's house. "I just...I fucked up so badly with Bobby and I think he just broke up with me-"

"I thought that was the plan."

"It was, but then...we fell in love. Like for real."

"Well, that man has loved you for forever."

"And I'm just figuring it out and I might...I might be too late."

"Oh, honey, love is never too late. You know how you know?"

"How?"

"Because you call a friend in the middle of the night crying because you're scared you might be too late. You know because you know."

I stopped on the sidewalk in front of my mother's house, the truth like a lightning bolt across my whole soul. I know because I know. I love him because I do. It's real because it is.

"Thank you, Vanessa."

"No problem."

We hung up and I climbed the cement steps to my mother's side door and knocked before pushing it open and stepping into her warm familiar kitchen, only to see silver fox Scott Morrison sitting at my old kitchen table, with a beer in front of him. My mother sitting across from him with wide, surprised eyes.

"Mari!"

"Mom?"

"Hi Mari," Scott said. "Merry Christmas."

"Hi Scott. Same to you."

"What are you doing here, honey?' Mom asked, getting to her feet. She wore trim black pants and a green sweater she saved for events. It was a date outfit. Mom was on a date. "Is everything all right?"

"Yes," I said, giving her a big smile. My life was total shit, but Mom's was absolutely going all right and I wasn't about to derail that for a moment. "I'm just...do you have any of my art stuff?"

"Of course. It's in your room. I can-"

"I got it, Mom. You just keep on, keeping on."

My room was directly opposite my brother's old room and when I opened it the smell of high school – the smell of me in high school, wafted out. Oil paint, linseed oil and Bath and Body Works Sweat Pea lotion.

I had a stack of unused canvases and my old oils case. I grabbed some rags and my jar of brushes and took as much as I could carry back through to the kitchen.

"Honey," Mom said, looking at me loaded down with all my old stuff. "Do you need a ride?"

"Nope," I said. Though, of course I did, but I was not pulling my mother out of this moment for the life of me. "Mom, I love you." I kissed her cheek. "See you in the morning. Scott..." I turned to him, sitting in the chair that always sat empty in our kitchen. I liked the way he filled the corner and the way his eyes sparkled when they looked over my shoulder at my mom.

"Yes?"

"Don't be a dick."

"I won't," he said, the smile gone from his face. "I promise."

Good enough for me.

I walked out of my childhood home with everything I'd left behind, and took it back to my spot above the bakery.

The oils were old and a little tight, but loosened up with some work. I set the largest canvas on my kitchen table, propped up with books and my stand mixer. What did I want to paint?

What did...?

The image came to me in rich gold colors with shades of blue and red and I spent no time thinking about it. I just started to work. I was rusty and my hands were clumsy. The connections between my brain and my body were not as sharp as they'd been when I'd been painting every day, but those too got loosened up with some work. I made the perfect blue. I made the perfect green.

Shades of gold.

I set aside that canvas to dry and found a smaller one for another image. The more I worked, the more I wanted to work. Years of work poured out of me. It wasn't until the sun was coming up and the canvases were full, that I took a step back and saw everything. The whole picture. This time my tears were happy.

All of it, every image, was Bobby.

~

BOBBY

I WENT over to my parent's house early because I couldn't stand my apartment anymore. I couldn't stand to be alone with my sadness anymore. If I couldn't be with Mari, I could be with people who loved me and their tofu.

"Hey, son!" Dad said as I came in with a good bottle of scotch. "You're early." He kissed me on both cheeks as was his way, and hugged me like it might be the last time.

"I am, is that okay? I was just kicking around my house-"

"Hi, honey!" Pop came in, cleaning off his glasses. He had cranberry splatter across the whole of him. "Had a little cranberry mishap. But everything is fine." He put his glasses on. "Where's Mari?"

Right. I had to do this. I had to say the words out loud.

"She..." I trailed off because I didn't know what to say. How to make sense of what happened. That was the beauty of parents. My Dads took one look at my heart and wrapped their arms around me.

"Should I open that Jameson's?" Dad asked.

I nodded against his shoulder.

"Does this mean there won't be any dessert?" Pop asked in a whisper.

"Bruce!" Dad cried.

"I'm just asking!" Pop stepped back, hands up. "I need to check on dinner, but you open that bottle and come into the kitchen and talk to me."

That's how I ended up getting drunk with my dads on Christmas Eve.

"So," Dad said, his grey hair standing on end. He drank his Jameson's out of a coffee mug I made him in junior high. "You're saying you broke up with her?"

"What was I supposed to do?" I asked. Pop burned the tofu, so we were eating mashed potatoes, straight out of the casserole dish.

"I don't know?" Pop said. He was drinking his Jameson's in a champagne glass, and had been outraged on Mari's behalf for thirty minutes. "Give her some time?"

"Yeah," I said. "You're probably right."

"Of course, I'm right," Pop said. "aren't I, Ed?"

"You usually are," Dad said, and leaned over to kiss Pop's cheek. Pop smiled at Dad and they forgot about me for a second, the way they sometimes did, and just smiled at each other. It was, without a doubt, one of the sweetest things about them. Was I wrong to want that? Was I wrong to want to be loved as much as I loved?

No.

Was I wrong to want it on my timeline? When the person I loved was living through some shit and maybe needed a minute to get her bearings?

Yes.

"So, what do I do?" I asked. The Jameson's and the sleepless night and mashed potatoes were making a mess of my decision-making skills.

"Grovel."

"Yeah, big grovel."

"Now?" I asked, and was already getting to my feet. "I should go find her now." I wanted to go find her now. I hadn't seen her for a day and I missed her. I missed her so much.

"Well," they looked at each other. "You're not at your best, son. You probably want to be at your best."

"Right." I sat back down.

There was a knock at the door and we all looked at each other blankly. "Are you expecting anyone?" Pop asked Dad.

Dad shrugged and poured more Jameson's in everyone's odd ball glass.

"Hello!" someone called out, and my heart spiked in my chest.

"Is that Mari?" Dad whispered.

"I think it is," Pop whispered back.

"Mari?" I said, and I got to my feet just as she came

walking into the kitchen. It was like a flashback. Mari had paint all over her hands, and some on her neck. The clothes she'd been wearing last night were rumpled and stained with paint. Her hair was at extreme Mari levels. There were three paintbrushes tucked into the bun at the back of her head.

"Hi!" She said, looking like a firecracker going off in a night sky. "I hope I'm not interrupting." We all looked down at the casserole dish we'd been eating mashed potatoes out of. There were three forks, no plates. A jar of pickles and a half bottle of whiskey.

"I burned the tofu," Pop said, like that explained everything.

"Are you three drunk?" she asked, like she was delighted.

"Well, Bobby got his heart broken last night," Dad said, sitting back with his arms crossed over his barrel chest. My defender to the end.

"Calm down, Dad," I said. "What are you doing here?" I asked Mari. "And...have you slept?"

"No," she said. "No. I haven't. I am here because I want to show you something. Can I..." I stepped forward as if to follow her to some place private to talk, but she held up her hand. "I meant, can I borrow your living room for a second and you stay in here and don't come in until I say it's okay? I know, weird ask, but I don't know, I'm only going to do this once in my life, so I want to do it right."

Pop all but pushed me down in my chair. "I'll keep an eye on him," he said. His glasses getting a little foggy again because he was probably going to cry.

"Wonderful. Ed? Could you help me?"

Oh, brave choice going with the hard line dad and not the pushover, but she knew what she was getting into. Dad stood, hit his head on the light over the kitchen table and shuffle-walked around the table to stand in front of her.

"Thank you," she said and the two of them vanished. There was some thumping. Dad swore. Something broke.

"It's fine!" Dad shouted.

Pop and I smiled at each other.

"You love her?" Pop asked quietly.

"So much."

"Okay!" Mari said, coming back into the kitchen, Dad behind her, wiping his eyes. Ah, whatever was in there was good, if it got him tearing up.

"You all right?" I asked him.

"I'm good, son." He said, wrapping his arm around Pop's waist. "I'm good. Go on in."

"So," Mari said, standing in the doorway, twisting her fingers together. "You asked last night if I missed anything from my old life. If I wished I was living that life and not this one. I couldn't answer because, I did miss some parts of my old life. I did miss who I was before Jake pulled me to pieces. I miss art. I miss being an artist. I miss it so much. But I don't miss the city. I don't miss that life. I just want to be here, but I want to be an artist again. And not in a bakery kind of way, though I love my job and I'm not quitting, but, I want to paint again."

"Good, you should," I said quietly.

"Last night I went and got all my old supplies. I spent the whole night painting. The whole night just downloading these images and moments in my head onto the canvas. I was so happy. Not just because I was painting, which I love. But I was painting someone I loved – which is you."

She stepped out of the way, and there, propped up on the couch and dad's recliner and in front of the TV, were a dozen canvases. Images of me.

Just my hands in one. Me walking away with Nora on my shoulders, a blurry winter carnival around us. A brilliant blue eye, that I guessed was mine. Mistletoe. Then one big one that was just color. A sky at morning, blues and golds and pinks. Green at the bottom. Hints of red at the top. It was a painting, when you looked at it, that took your breath away. That filled you with big feelings that were hard to name. Beauty where it turned a little bit to love. Hope where it turned to faith. Sorrow where it turned to joy.

"What is that?" I asked.

"The way you make me feel," she whispered. Behind us there was some loud sniffing. "I love you. I think I always have. It's been you, Bobby, all along. I'm sorry I made you doubt for even a second, when you've been so amazing and patient." She lowered her voice. "Also the sex has been so good and I've been weird and prickly and-"

"Perfect," I interrupted her. "You've been perfect, Mari. There's no other way for you to be."

I smiled at her, drunk and in love and so happy in the moment I felt like I could explode.

"Oh my god, you idiot, kiss her," Dad said.

So, I did.

I kissed her and Dad and Pop cheered and then went back into the kitchen. Mari kissed me back, and as far as moments in my life went, this was perfect. The best one yet.

"I'm not done," she said.

"There's more art?"

"Not art, but I was going to take you on a Christmas date."

"Oh really?" I asked.

"I borrowed a sled from the Okinde's. I want to take you sledding."

"No, you don't."

"No. I do. I really do. It'll be fun."

"How about this?" I said, and reached for my coat that I'd thrown over the back of the couch. "We go back to your place and I let you take advantage of me in my drunken state."

"Oh, I like where this is going."

"Then we both take a much-needed nap."

"Tell me more."

"And then we go sledding."

"It's Christmas tomorrow," she said.

I pushed a wild curl off her face. "It is."

"I think...you're my Christmas present."

"I know you are mine."

We invited my dads over to Mari's mom's house for dinner tomorrow night. "Scott Morrison might be there."

"The writer?" I asked.

"It's a long story, I'll tell you later." She turned to my parents, who, I could tell, were nearly melting with early onset hangovers and joy. "The food isn't great, but the desserts are amazing and we'd...we'd just love to have you."

"We'd love to come." There were hugs all around.

"I'll be back for the paintings," she said.

"Oh, can we keep the one of his eye? The colors are perfect."

"Like a Vermeer," I said, and Mari gasped, her hands clasped to her face. "Oh calm down, I've picked up a couple things hanging out with you. Come on. Take me home."

We walked out of my parent's house and into a Christmas Eve and a future that felt nothing short of magical.

"I love you," she said. "I believe in you. You're my fairy tale. My happily ever after."

"I love you too. I have forever and I will forever."

EPILOGUE

Bobby

"I think maybe this is one of those things that's only fun when you're a kid," Mari said, standing at the top of the sledding hill at Conservation Park. We were surrounded by kids who were trying out new sleds Santa left under the tree.

"No," I said. "I think sledding is one of those things that is always fun. Like getting chased with a squirt gun."

"That's fun?"

"What kind of childhood did you have, Mari?"

"You know what was fun as a kid?" She asked, tugging her red hat down over her ears. This Christmas morning was icy cold and bright. "Getting your book checkout limit extended at the library."

"Oh yeah," I said, remembering that kind of bliss. "That is fun. But so is this. I promise."

"We don't have helmets," she said. "These kids have helmets."

"Hey, Mike Watson!" I said to one of the teenagers who was there with his younger brothers. "Can we borrow two helmets?"

Suddenly Mari was wearing a bright pink helmet with a unicorn horn on it, and I had a rather cool black helmet with Thrasher on the side.

"We look ridiculous," she said.

"Yep. Stop stalling. I've been wanting to go sledding with you for about twenty years, so let's get going."

She melted every time I reminded her how long I've loved her. After our earth-shattering sex last night, with the addition of her vibrator, and our post sex nap, we ordered pizza and she asked me to tell her the minute I fell for her.

"There was no minute," I said. "There were millions of them."

I told her about that time in biology class when the sun came out from behind a cloud and she closed her eyes and tilted her face to the sun. When she came back from New York, different and intense, and I saw her for the first time at the bakery and she'd hugged me like she'd missed me.

"I remember that too," she'd said. "You walked in and it felt like the sun coming out after a bad storm."

What was a guy to do but reward such sweetness with more orgasms, putting off our sledding date a little bit longer.

However, there was no delaying the sledding date now. I sat down in the back of the red plastic sled and she got in between my legs and we both twined our legs together so we weren't dragging. I wrapped my hands around her waist, tucked my chin to her cheek. "You ready?"

"I guess."

I scooted us down the hill until we hit critical mass and we were sledding. And then...we were zooming down the hill. She started screaming. As we went faster, she gripped my hands and her screams turned to laughter. Snow was in our eyes and we were on the edge of control. We hit a bump and went flying into the air, both of us losing contact with the sled and falling, face first, into the big drifts of snow piled up at the bottom of the hill.

"Mari!" I said, pulling her upright, swiping the snow off her face. "You all right?"

She tackled me back into the snow. The cold seeping down into the collar of my jacket. She kissed my cold face with hot lips. "That was perfect. More fun than I remembered. Let's go again."

"Again," I agreed. Again. Forever.

∿

DID YOU ENJOY THIS NOVELLA? Want to stay tuned for upcoming releases and bonus material? Join our newsletter!

Newsletter Sign Up!

ALSO BY HAILEY SHORE

Happily Ever Maybe?

Not My Prince Charming

The Grump, The Bride & The Baby

Printed in Great Britain
by Amazon

27519350R00099